Furious, he grabbed her arm. Tightening his hold on her, he pulled the car off the road, scooted across the seat, and grabbing her ponytail, yanked her head backwards and screamed into her face,

"What have you been wearing to work? How have you been behaving toward the male employees? What do they say to you and worse yet, what do *you say to them?*"

Kendra could not believe this was happening to her. All of her life, she had tried to do what God and her family instructed her to do. She had tried to live by the rules in the Scriptures, and although she knew she wasn't perfect, she *did* know that she *wasn't guilty of anything to cause these calls. In fact, it was just the opposite.* She worked very hard to keep her reputation and conscience clean. Now he was making her feel that the phone calls were *her fault*! Her head ached from the force of the jerk on her neck and her arm was throbbing. She could see bruises where his fingers held her arm. She began to cry.

"And stop crying," he yelled. And he slapped her face. Then just as suddenly as he exploded, he reached out, put his arms around her, and pulled her against him. The blackness in his eyes receded like ocean water recedes when the tide goes out, and in its place she saw once again the soft brown, gentle eyes of the Keith she had come to love.

"There, baby," he said, untying her hair ribbon, allowing the mass of ringlets to fall around her shoulders.

What They Are Saying About
The Passing Of Paradise

The Passing of Paradise takes readers from the bliss of love to the abuse of a spouse. Written with compassion and Christian insights, this story examines a difficult situation in the light of the Word of God.

Kendra's unsophisticated innocence will touch readers' hearts. The author has dramatically contrasted the good and the evil. Eloquent writing and well-defined characters take this issue to the minds of readers, as they wonder what Kendra will decide. God's Word on the subject of marriage is quoted and discussed in the context of the story. There are a series of twists and turns that will alternately surprise and shock readers. An interesting touch was setting the story in the 1950's. There were more taboos against divorce during that time, which made it an even more difficult decision.

The Passing of Paradise was a well-written book about an often unspoken sin.

—Joyce Handzo
Dancing Word Reviewer

Wings

The Passing Of Paradise

by

Molly Lemmons

A Wings ePress, Inc.

Inspirational Women's Fiction

Wings ePress, Inc.

Edited by: Lorraine Stephens
Copy Edited by: Sara Reinke
Senior Editor: Lorraine Stephens
Executive Editor: Lorraine Stephens
Cover Artist: Christine Poe

Wings ePress Books
http://www.wings-press.com

Copyright © 2005 by Molly Lemmons
ISBN 1-59088-578-3

Published In the United States Of America

April 2005

Wings ePress Inc.
403 Wallace Court
Richmond, KY 40475

Dedication

To my precious grandchildren, Fredric (Ric) and Carlotta (Carly) who have brought so much joy into my life, I cannot even describe it, and for whom I pray will someday search carefully so that they will find a paradise that will never "pass."

Prologue

The blinding snow hit Kendra's face with a stinging force as she struggled to walk along the deserted road. The ferocity of the Oklahoma wind, coupled with the driving snow made it almost impossible for her to stand, much less walk. What would she do if she could not locate a farmhouse or someone to help her? Her new white 1954 Chevrolet Bel Air her father gave her for graduation was behind her at least a quarter of a mile. She had been lucky to get out of it after she had hit the ice that had plummeted it down the embankment and into the ditch.

Her hands, even in warm mittens, continued to throb with pain. *Thank goodness*, she thought, *I left the house with my warm clothes on.* She knew she should not be out here so late at night in such a terrible snowstorm. Her car—the same color as the snow covering—would never be found before the snow melted, she reasoned, and that may be days, even weeks away. It didn't snow often in Oklahoma, but when it did; it could freeze and stay frozen for days, even after the snow stopped. And now it was pitch dark, and the falling snow was becoming deeper as the wind swept it into large drifts beside the road.

She wondered if the drifts would obstruct her view and she would never know if indeed, a farmhouse *was even there*. Terror filled Kendra's heart, and the tears streaming down her cheeks were beginning to freeze as numbness set in. "Oh, my little Millie!" she cried aloud as the culmination of all the memories leading her to this predicament became more vivid. With every determined step she took onto the crunchy, now freezing snow beneath her feet, she realized that she could no longer refuse to acknowledge the pain. It was *real* and it *did* happen...

Please, God, she prayed... *Help me...*

One

Kendra Tinker was beautiful. Her striking features, coupled with her kindness, easy laughter, and genuine interest in others, caused those who knew her to love her for her inner beauty as well. Of Irish and Indian descent, Kendra had the olive skin and large, translucent, dark brown eyes of her half-Cherokee Indian father, and the reddish, golden hair of her Irish mother. A combination so striking, and so uncommon, Kendra was often subjected to, and embarrassed by, the stares of others. Her thick, long lashes arched over her huge eyes, and sparkled in a rim of golden red lights. Her waist-long hair, swirling around her face in lazy, relaxed ringlets, framed it like a golden halo ablaze with fire. Her petite frame gave her a delicate appearance that seemed to beg for protection.

She met Keith Kouch at a church social. He was dashing and handsome with thick black hair and deep, penetrating brown eyes. Those eyes pierced her with an indescribable mystery, and she could not look away. There was magnetism about them that she could not understand, but she was compelled to try. He was strong, of athletic build, muscular and self-confident, and the broad smile that flashed quickly across his face revealed his flawless teeth. The blaring whiteness of them stood out in contrast to his tan face. Kendra looked small and vulnerable beside him, and her gentle, loving disposition seemed to add a dimension of intrigue to Keith Kouch, causing him to be interested in more than just meeting her.

"Hi," he greeted her. "I'm Keith Kouch. I'm new here." And he smiled a smile that caused Kendra's big brown eyes to mist, and her heart to race. He clasped her hand in his, greeting her with a firm handshake, her small hand disappearing inside his massive palm.

For the duration of the party, the two were together.

"May I take you home?' he asked her as the party drew to an end. Kendra wanted to have him take her home more than she had ever wanted anything, but with her car in the shop, her parents were probably already on their way to get her and so it was too late to call them not to come.

"That's okay," Keith told her. "May I see you tomorrow?"

Kendra hesitated only a moment before answering, "That would be nice."

The next day, bright and early on Saturday morning, the phone rang in Kendra's room, waking her from a deep sleep. The ring startled Millie, her white Persian kitten who had been asleep by Kendra's side, and she jumped like a little ping-pong ball of fur, lost her balance, and fell off the bed. "Oh, Millie, you're so silly!" she giggled as she picked up the phone. It was Keith.

"What's so funny that you're laughing this early in the morning?"

"Oh, my little Millie is so funny... The ring scared her and she fell off the bed!"

Keith got right to the point of the call. Could she go with him to the park and walk through the botanical gardens, and visit the museum on the premises?

"I would love to go to the park with you, Keith." After hanging up the phone, she rolled out of bed, gathered up her long locks with a shiny, satin ribbon and with her ecru lace nightgown flowing behind her, grabbed one of the posts on her bed. Breaking out in song, she twirled and floated from one post to another, turning and twisting, and dancing until her heart was pounding. Millie sat on the edge of the bed, her tail swishing from side to side, and her eyes round as marbles as she watched Kendra's every move. Millie was actually a grown cat, but Kendra called her a kitten because she was so small.

A Christmas present from her father the year she turned sixteen, she was the best gift Kendra ever received.

Remembering the little box as it sat under the tree with holes punched in it and tied with a blue satin ribbon made Kendra smile. When she had opened the box, a pair of azure blue eyes, and a motor the sound of a thunder rumble had greeted her. There had been instant bonding between the two.

"Guess what, Millie? I get to go out with Keith Kouch! What do you think of that?" She scratched Millie under the chin, as the kitten purred her contentment and began to knead her paws into the blue satin comforter.

Kendra spoke to her parents about meeting Keith at the party, and they too, were anxious to meet him. Brought up in a home amidst high moral standards, Kendra was well aware of the importance of having her parents get acquainted with Keith. An obedient child, she had grown up under the rule and thumb of a stern, but loving father, and a kind, affectionate mother. She was reared with strict guidelines of behavior and she set goals for herself that she followed intently. Unskilled in the art of "dating," and a bit naïve and innocent, Kendra led a protective life; indeed, a part of her incredible beauty was her unsophisticated innocence.

Kendra reached for her robe hanging on the back of her vanity chair and tied it around her waist. Just as she started to run down the stairs, she stopped a second, then on an impulse, slid down the banister, singing all the way. Millie bobbed along down the stairs beside her as she slid.

"And what has made my little daughter so happy this morning?" her mother asked with a twinkle in her eye as Kendra went into the breakfast nook.

"Oh, Mom, Keith asked me to go to the park and visit the museum this afternoon. I am sooo excited! I can't wait for you and Daddy to meet him!"

"Well, he must really be someone special to cause you such excitement and happiness," her mother replied. Kendra ate her breakfast, helped to clear the table, then headed back upstairs to clean her room, finish her homework, and, time permitting, practice the piano. Until now the piano and her music had been her first love. An accomplished pianist and vocalist, Kendra planned to pursue a career in music. When she wasn't practicing the piano, she was singing and most of the time, doing *both*. She enjoyed a God-given talent for music and it had shown itself from the very beginning of her young life.

Her long, slender fingers floated without any effort on her part over the piano keys and the beautiful sounds drifted all through the house. She played for hours, never tiring of it. Her dream had been to own a baby grand piano, and when she had raked in all the competitive honors possible in music, her father had surprised her with the realization of that dream.

When she practiced, Millie always joined her on the piano bench. She listened as she sat very still, with only the movement of her tail swishing side to side as it hung off the bench. And the kitten sat for as long as it took. When Kendra finished playing, Millie walked down the keyboard; satisfied that she could show Kendra that she, *too,* could "play" it. To have received Millie as a surprise from her father at Christmas that year had been to Kendra as wonderful as receiving the baby grand piano.

As a little girl, she had sung all of the time, and being such a quick learner, she had played the piano at a very early age. She was a junior at Oklahoma City University, known for its superior music department, and her time to develop this talent had never had any competition—that is, *until now.*

At precisely 2:00 the doorbell rang. *Exactly on time,* Kendra thought, as she bounced down the stairs.

After much thought, she had chosen to wear her copper-colored silk skirt and her peach-colored silk blouse with the flutter ruffle at the neck. She wanted to look *just right.* As she flung open the door, the sun streamed into the room, bathing her in a bright radiance of gold. Her silky curls, shining like little copper springs bounced softly around her shoulders, and a glittering golden barrette held them in place.

"Hi, Keith, please come in. I want you to meet my parents."

Kendra's father, sitting in his recliner in his study, was reading the newspaper when the two entered. Kenneth Tinker could appear very intimidating. He was a large boned man of stout structure, and he was tall and handsome. His eyes were as black as his hair, and his smooth, flawless complexion was the color of a cup of hot coffee with a hefty dose of thick cream. An adoring family man, he was deeply respected and held in the highest esteem by the pharmaceutical company for which he worked as a pharmacist.

Kenneth Tinker was the head of his family and the major decision-maker. Even though he sometimes appeared to be too stern, the motives behind every decision he made were for the good of his family, and they all knew it. Not one of them ever doubted his love. Nell's love for him was so deep that being in total subjection to him was a joy because she felt the love and protection he gave her in return. Kendra deeply respected her father and lived by his rules in a constant effort to always please him.

Upon seeing Keith and Kendra enter the study, he put the paper aside. As he did so, Keith strolled over and extended his hand.

"I'm glad to meet you, Mr. Tinker."

Kendra could tell that her father was "sizing up" this young man. He did not say a word, and he withheld his hand for what seemed an eternity to Kendra. Nell Tinker interrupted the awkward silence when she walked into the room. Still wearing her white, starched apron with the ruffle on the hem and an oven mitt on her hand, she was gracious and kind for her daughter's sake, whose uneasiness she sensed. It was obvious where Kendra got her sweet disposition.

Nell was a dainty lady with long, slender legs and porcelain white skin. A few faint freckles that managed to dodge the shade of her sunbonnet dotted her turned-up nose, and her autumn-auburn hair bounced when she walked as it swung around her ears. Her bluebonnet-blue eyes, laced with tiny white flecks like miniature snowflakes, danced with happiness. Her face seemed always to be ready to smile and her optimistic nature, quick wit, and sense of humor made her a magnet to a host of friends.

"Hi, Keith, I'm Nell, and all is well," she quipped as she grasped Keith's hand with the oven mitt in a cordial handshake that made up for her husband's temporary loss of manners.

"Oops! I'm sorry for the mitt," she said, taking it off and offering another handshake to the now perplexed young man standing before her. Nell thought she saw a darkness pass over Keith's eyes that, for an instant, made her uneasy. Her momentary distraction was interrupted, however, and soon forgotten when the door to the study flew open and Kendra's two little sisters and brother all rushed in, eager to meet "sister's new boyfriend!" Kendra blushed and turned away so that Keith couldn't see her embarrassment.

It was time for Kenneth Tinker to speak. "Well, now, Keith, what do you do *for fun?* Do you like to hunt or fish? Play golf? What are your hobbies?" He stood up and it was as though he was in slow motion as he took his time to light his pipe. Then leaning against his desk, he crossed his legs, folded his arms, and waited for answers. And they were the right ones. The older man finally extended his hand in friendship.

Kendra's siblings, a hand clasped over their mouths to stifle giggles, read with accuracy the message in their mother's stern glance, and tiptoed out.

It wasn't long before the two men were chattering like magpies about the upcoming fall season of quail hunting. At this point, Keith had himself an ally: they both loved to hunt quail and both owned an English Setter bird dog. Kendra knew now that Keith had won her father's heart. She would later ask her mother if it was possible to know whom you would marry after meeting him the first time.

When she could drag Keith out of her father's study, they left for the park. It was a perfect day—not a cloud in the clear blue sky and no wind, which was unusual for that time of year in Oklahoma. They walked through the botanical gardens, then to the museum where they learned they shared a mutual interest in the arts.

Back home, Kenneth and Nell discussed the young man who seemed to have won their eldest child's heart. "There's something about his eyes," Nell wondered aloud, then the thought was lost with the same ease it had entered her mind.

At the park, Kendra and Keith circled the pond, then sat down on the grass. Swans were swimming lazily back and forth in front of them as they talked of many things. They found they had much in common, that they could discuss all issues of life, and they were comfortable with one another. And just as Kendra expected, Keith was the perfect gentleman, courteous and polite.

As the sinking sun began to cast evening shadows across them, Keith knew it was time to leave. But first, they would stop to get a bite to eat at the corner drive-in. This gave them more time to talk, too. Kendra's stomach was so full of butterflies, all she could order was an orange slush, her favorite, but she didn't mind when Keith ordered a burger and fries.

The outside speakers were playing songs from *Your Hit Parade*, and as the beautiful lyrics of *My Prayer* by *The Platters* began to play, Kendra, in her excitement, turned to Keith.

"Oh, Keith, that's my favorite song! Let's pick up the same station and synchronize the car radio with it for a stereo effect!" And her eyes danced with anticipation as she looked up at Keith. His brown eyes suddenly deepened to a black, unlike anything Kendra had ever seen, and his neck began to turn red, the color growing in intensity from his collarbone up to the top of his face. As she reached to turn the knob, an angry Keith slapped her hand with such a forceful thrust that her hand stung with pain. "I'll operate the radio... *You* will *not*!" he yelled. And the pulsating veins in his neck stood out as if they would burst.

Shocked by this outburst of temper, Kendra moved away and folded her hands in her lap, so stunned she couldn't speak. Tears began to build in her eyes, and just as suddenly as Keith's temper flared, it subsided. His eyes returned to their usual soft brown, the red receded from his neck, and changing the subject was as abrupt as the outbreak. Not once did he mention how he had hurt her.

In fact, the return to "normal" was so swift that Kendra began to think she had imagined what had just happened. Indeed, in time, she would convince herself of that; therefore, she did not give it another thought.

Keith looked at his watch and realized that it was almost 11:00; the time he had promised to have Kendra home. They had been talking for nearly four hours and neither had realized how late it was.

From Lawton, Oklahoma, Keith faced about a two and half-hour drive to get back home. He and his family would soon be moving to Oklahoma City where they would be attending the church the Tinker family had attended all of their lives.

Keith's father was retiring from the military, and his mother, after twenty-four years of teaching, had already retired. A domineering and rigid father, Cal Kouch was strict and cold as steel when the Kouch children were growing up. No matter what decision he made, he felt he was never wrong, and he never negotiated a compromise under any circumstances. He was a large man—six-foot-eight, two hundred and seventy-five pounds—and he stood ramrod straight. He had thick, wavy black hair, heavy eyebrows, and a thick, immaculately groomed mustache, giving him a stern, disapproving look.

Edwina Kouch was an independent, powerful woman who looked beyond her husband's controlling personality, and loved him anyway. His late night evenings of not being at home, when his whereabouts were questionable, were not things she allowed herself to think about. She was secure with who she was, and she understood Cal, perhaps better than he understood himself. She was the one who absorbed the blows of inconsistencies in her husband's mannerisms, and was always there to soften the sometimes cruel and unjust decisions that were made regarding their three children. She was a plump little lady with rosy cheeks, big blue eyes and short, curly brown hair that hugged her head like a little skullcap. Despite her situation, which could cause her great unhappiness, laughter came easily for her, and she never let life get her down. She was the "heart" of their home and she made life bearable for the children. Keith was the youngest child and the twins, Kayla and Kyle had both finished college. Kayla was married, and teaching school over in Arkansas. Once she left home, she seldom came back; however, she called her mother daily. Kyle was drafted into the army right out of high school, and like his father, had chosen it for his career. Of all three children, he was most like his father. Having escaped the draft, Keith often felt he had disappointed his father by not enlisting. This was an extra baggage of guilt that he seemed to always carry with him.

A "late in life" baby, Keith was spoiled and pampered by his older siblings and they adored him. As a small boy, he was even-tempered, sensitive, and gentle, often causing him to be the recipient of taunting and teasing when he started to school. He was called a "sissy," and girls made fun of his gentle nature. Not interested in playing football, to his father's disgust, he often fell victim to his taunting,

"What's a matter, Son, can't you take it?" his father would ask him, sneering.

When Keith was in the eighth grade, he had had enough, and with tremendous self-control, he began to lift weights regularly and faithfully. No girl would *ever* make fun of him again. As a result, by the time he began the ninth grade, he had developed the strong, muscular physique that had brought him to Kendra's attention the first time she saw him. She found the combination of a gentle spirit, housed in steel, to be nothing short of fascinating and exciting. Add all of that to his good looks, his strong interest in the church and spiritual matters, and Kendra felt sure she had met "Mr. Right."

Keith got out of the car to go around to the other side to open Kendra's door, and this thought went through Kendra's head: *He has it all: spirituality, good looks, kindness, and strength—what more could a girl want or need?*

"Kendra, I had a wonderful time today," he told her as they walked up to the front porch. "I hope you will let me call you again," and he brushed a ringlet of reddish, golden hair from her cheek. His eyes were soft and kind, and his touch, gentle.

"That would be nice," Kendra replied. "I had a wonderful time, too. Thank you." And she turned to walk in. Before Keith could say anything, on another one of Kendra's impulses, she turned around and took hold of his hand. She gave it a quick squeeze, dropped it as suddenly as she had taken it, opened the door, and vanished behind it. Once inside, she scooped up the waiting Millie into her arms and hugged the kitten to her cheek. "Oh, Millie, isn't he just wonderful?" And the kitten purred.

That was the beginning of what Kendra hoped would turn into a deep friendship and finally, love. Sunday morning came and Keith sat beside her in church. He didn't sing the hymns because he said he liked to remain silent and listen to *her* beautiful voice. When the song leader led "Count Your Many Blessings," Kendra looked up at Keith and whispered, "I *am* counting, and *you're number one!*"

Monday morning came and Kendra had to get ready for her 8:00 a.m. college algebra class. She wasn't in the mood. She wanted to stay in bed and dream, but had to get moving. She had come too far to quit now, and her dream of being a music teacher must be realized. Her mother had warned her that she would always regret it if she didn't finish what she had started.

She knew her mother was right; it was just that something was diverting her interest right now, and that "something" was named *Keith*.

Two

Spring quickly turned into summer, as Kendra wrapped up her third year of study at OCU. Now that she was out for the summer, her part-time job in downtown Oklahoma City would become full-time. But she still had time for Keith, who was becoming more and more of an influence in her life. They were together almost constantly, often playing Forty-Two with Kenneth and Nell until late into the night, or popping corn and working crossword puzzles. Sometimes, he sat beside her when she played the piano and he sang along with her.

Most people were buying televisions now that they were becoming so popular, but Kenneth just wanted to have the family doing *things together*, so he said he would put off buying one for a while longer.

Kendra's cashier's desk at work was located in the basement of Brown's Department Store in downtown Oklahoma City. The phone was a busy one. The store closed at 5:30 daily except on Monday nights when it stayed open until 8:30. Kendra was allowed to park her car in the alley behind the store where other employees kept their cars. It was off the street and no other cars were allowed to park there. At 8:25 one Monday evening, as Kendra was closing the cash register, the phone rang.

"Brown's Basement," Kendra answered. The voice on the other end asked to speak to Kendra. "This is Kendra," she said, beginning to feel a little uneasy.

"Do you know what I would like to do to you?" the voice asked, whispering and breathing heavily. "I know that you drive a 1954 white Chevrolet Bel Air and I know where it's parked. I'll wait for you in the alley." And with a deep, heavy sigh, he hung up.

Judy McClure, a woman in her late forties was the desk manager who had personally hired Kendra. She was a "bottle-red-head" with a temper to match her dyed hair, and she had been "around the block a time or two." Judy was a coarse woman with thick, dry, prematurely wrinkled skin from chain smoking since she had been twelve, and she was struggling to keep her sixth marriage together. When she had hired Kendra, she had seen in her a part of what she had once longed to be.

Judy could not have children; therefore, her natural, motherly instincts were poured out on Kendra and she placed a protective shield around her at all times, constantly watching to see that no harm came to her, and that no one spoiled her sweet, innocent nature.

When she saw Kendra's trembling hand replace the phone on its cradle, and saw the tears start to fall, she went over to her and asked, "What's the matter, darlin'?"

Kendra was trembling so hard that Judy had to put her arm around her to steady her. The girl was terrified. "Tell me dear," she said, her voice gentle and kind.

Kendra told Judy what the man had said and Judy flew into a rage. Her face became the color of her hair and she pounded the desk. "Just makes me furious! They always pick on the innocent... We'll just *see* about this!" she yelled. And she stomped off to find Roy Brown, the House Detective.

The whistle blew, signaling 8:30, and the voice on the intercom announced, "The store is now closed." The building emptied almost as quickly as the announcement was made, and the main lights, on automatic timers, went out. Roy came to the desk and asked Kendra exactly what had been said and how the voice had sounded, and if it was a voice that she could identify if she heard it again.

Of course she couldn't. She was scared to death. Roy and Judy walked Kendra to her car and stayed until she had driven out of sight. Later that night, Kendra told her father about the incident.

"Kendra, the world is full of crazies; don't show your fear. From now on, I'll take you and pick you up from work. You can come straight out the front door and I'll be waiting."

The next day, Roy called an early store meeting and instructed the operators of the switchboard to monitor any calls going to the basement desk beginning that day. Roy would walk the floors of the store and watch for anything or anyone suspicious.

For the next few weeks, things were going along all right. Kenneth picked up his daughter at the door each day, and after awhile, the memory of the experience began to fade. Judy and Roy both went back to their regular routines, and Kendra managed to put it all behind her.

A few weeks later, one Tuesday night, the phone again rang—this time at 5:25, just five minutes before closing.

"Hey, little girl," the voice began, "I see your daddy picks you up every day. That changes nothing. I want to do a lot of things to you! For starters, I would like to turn you upside-down and..." Kendra slammed down the receiver and broke into tears.

Without a moment's hesitation, Judy called the operators. They were very apologetic, but they had forgotten to monitor the call; after all, it had been *weeks* since the first call.

Roy Brown was *livid. "You monitor every day!"* He ordered, wanting to be sure that his instructions were followed to the letter.

The next day, when the phone rang at five minutes before closing, Judy motioned for Kendra to answer it. It was *Keith*! The operators were on the monitor just as they had been told to be.

"Hi, Kendra. I'm coming to town this evening and I told your dad that I would pick you up. I thought we could go eat at Beverly's Chicken in the Rough, then go to the Cooper Theater. It begins at 8:00 and *Seven Brides for Seven Brothers* is on. It is a musical that I know you will enjoy!"

"Yes, I would, Keith. Isn't Jane Powell in it?"

"Yes, so you know the music will be great!"

When Kendra hung up the phone, Judy breathed a sigh of relief for Kendra. She just wished the operators would monitor when they were supposed to monitor.

Keith was waiting for Kendra at the door just as the store was closing, and she bounced out to the car, beaming, with Roy Brown close behind.

"Just wanted to be sure you were here, Keith. Gotta take care of this girl of ours, you know." And he opened the door for Kendra.

"Yeah, Roy thanks for your help." Then Roy went back into the store.

"I didn't realize that you knew Roy Brown, Keith."

"Yeah, we graduated together from Lawton High— been friends since grade school."

Keith looked at Kendra as he started the car and as usual, he thought she looked radiant. She was wearing her pale blue, circular skirt and peasant blouse with the triple row of ruffles around the neck. She was wearing her pale blue, satin ballerina slippers, and her hair was tied up in a cluster of bouncy curls with a pale blue ribbon to match.

Around her neck, she wore the tiny blue heart that he had given her when he had said, *"Just because... if I did, you would."* She was so glad to see him again. Their time had become so precious, each of them treasuring every moment they spent together.

They went to Beverly's Restaurant and shared a huge salad, and some "chicken in the rough." They had been sitting at the table a long while when Keith suddenly realized it was almost time for the show to start.

They jumped up, tossed the tip onto the table, and rushed out to the car. When they were almost to the theater, Keith, out of the blue, turned to Kendra and asked: "Kendra, your father tells me that you've been getting obscene phone calls at work. Is that right?"

Kendra had never told Keith about it for fear of worrying him. Her father, the police, Roy Brown and even Judy could handle it, she felt. Besides, it was not something that she wanted to talk about. It was embarrassing to her.

"Yes, Keith, that's right. I've been so scared." And she ached for Keith to take her hand and tell her it would be all right, that he would protect her at any cost, but he didn't.

Instead, she saw the dark look come into his eyes—the same one she had seen that night at Marlow's Drive In. Only this time, it deepened until his eyes were black pits, and she was seeing a person she didn't know.

Furious, he grabbed her arm. Tightening his hold on her, he pulled the car off the road, scooted across the seat, and grabbing her ponytail, yanked her head backwards and screamed into her face,

"What have you been wearing to work? How have you been behaving toward the male employees? What do they say to you and worse yet, what do *you say to them?*"

Kendra could not believe this was happening to her. All of her life, she had tried to do what God and her family instructed her to do. She had tried to live by the rules in the Scriptures, and although she knew she wasn't perfect, she *did* know that she *wasn't guilty of anything to cause these calls. In fact, it was just the opposite.* She worked very hard to keep her reputation and conscience clean. Now he was making her feel that the phone calls were *her fault*! Her head ached from the force of the jerk on her neck and her arm was throbbing. She could see bruises where his fingers held her arm. She began to cry.

"And stop crying," he yelled. And he slapped her face. Then just as suddenly as he exploded, he reached out, put his arms around her, and pulled her against him. The blackness in his eyes receded like ocean water recedes when the tide goes out, and in its place she saw once again the soft brown, gentle eyes of the Keith she had come to love.

"There, baby," he said, untying her hair ribbon, allowing the mass of ringlets to fall around her shoulders. Then, sorting them out one by one and twirling them around his fingers, he cooed, "Don't cry, sweetheart, I will take care of whoever is calling you. I will find him and I will assure you that he will never call again!"

Kendra sobbed into his shoulder and he continued to hold her until no more tears came. He took out his handkerchief and with soft pats, dried her eyes. Then holding her closer, he kissed her on the lips—the first time he had ever done that—and whispered in her ear, "Kendra, if I did ever love anyone, you would be the one. Always remember that: *If I did, you would."*

He had told her those words before, and she wondered exactly what he meant by them. Did he mean that it was hard for him to love anyone, but if he did, it would *be her*? Or did he mean that he would *never* love anyone, but if he did, it would be *her?* It was a thought she pushed into the back of her mind.

Keith slid back to the driver's side of the car and started it up. Kendra didn't speak for awhile. She just couldn't say anything. She had been hurt, both physically and emotionally, and she couldn't even think straight. She gathered her hair back up and tied the ribbon around it, and by the time they arrived at the picture show, all was back to normal. Keith was laughing and talking to her all over again, making her wonder if what had happened *really had happened. Was she losing her mind?*

There was no need to talk about it to Keith; he would only say that she "overreacted" and that it was only *because if he did love somebody, it would be her.*

Seven Brides for Seven Brothers was, as expected, a beautiful, uplifting musical, and Kendra's spirits were on the mend by the time it ended. Both of them were laughing and talking as they exited the theater and headed for the parking lot.

"I told you that would be good, didn't I? Of course, none of the music equals what *you* do, Kendra. No one has a more beautiful voice than *you*."

By the time Keith got Kendra home, all was forgotten. Any warning signs she may have seen were ignored. Her love for Keith was blinding her intellect.

Once at the door, Keith took Kendra by the shoulders and pulled her close. Holding her head in his hand, he ran his fingers through her hair and kissed her with tenderness on the cheek. Then he moved his lips to hers, and kissed her, holding her tight.

"Kendra," he mumbled, pressing his lips to her ears, "I want to marry you...someday."

Kendra felt her stomach turn to mush, and her legs grow weak, so she pulled away, and said, "Keith, I need to go in now. I want to marry you, too...someday." And she took both his hands in hers, kissed them, and quickly went inside, closing the door softly behind her.

"Is that you, Kendra?" her mother called from the den where she was waiting for her daughter to get home. Millie heard her voice and ran to greet her, her fluffy, "happy tail" sticking straight up behind her like a periscope.

"Yes, Mom... I'm home." Cradling Mille in her arms, she started up the stairs. She wanted to tell her mother about the evening, but it didn't seem important anymore. Keith was a wonderful man and she loved him—besides, she couldn't remember being all that upset. All she focused on was how sweet and loving he had been, and his kiss that had been Heaven to her. *He had the power to completely dislodge any memories that may not be pleasant, simply by being tender and kind to her.*

She floated upstairs in a lovesick trance, not once recalling the agony she had just suffered a few hours beforehand. She remembered only that Keith said he wanted to marry her someday and that if he did love someone, it would be her.

Marriage held a romantic intrigue to Kendra. Taught the Scriptures all of her life, that sex is to be held in high esteem, and for marriage only, she dreamed of the day she was saving for her husband. She believed virginity to be a gift to be given to her husband and opened only on their wedding night. She just knew that saving herself for that special occasion would be a marvelous, romantic experience, and it was these convictions that enabled her to maintain her purity. And with those romantic thoughts, she cuddled Millie close to her cheek, and the kitten's purring lulled her into a sound and peaceful sleep.

A week or so passed and Kendra did not receive any more of the threatening calls. She hoped that somehow the caller had gotten wind of the beefed up security precautions on the store phone monitors, and had been scared away.

But it was not to be. The phone rang again at 5:25 one Tuesday evening as the store was closing. Kendra answered it. It caught her off guard as she had begun to think she was safe.

"Kendra?" the breathless voice asked. "I know that you think I'm gone but I'm not. And I won't go away until I have you. Ohhhhhh, I have sooo many plans for you, my little Uppity Miss. When I get through with you, you won't be so high and mighty and such a goody-good—you *will beg me for more....*" Kendra had been instructed to hold him on the line as long as she could, so biting her lip, she held on to the receiver, tears spilling down her cheeks.

Judy recognized immediately what was happening and tore out the door. The elevator operators were shutting down their stations, and Judy knew that with the adrenaline flowing like hers was at that moment, she could get up there faster by running the stairs. Making four flights in a matter of minutes, she burst into the business office just as they were closing down.

"That call to the basement just now—-where did it come from?" she demanded.

The Chief Operator said, "Oh, I forgot to monitor. Let me check and see if the cord is still in that call slot."

A quick scan of the switchboard, showed that sure enough, the slot was still connected! Kendra had managed to keep him on line just long enough. With a hasty check of the number lists, the Chief Operator announced, "That call came from within the store!"

Immediately, security summoned for help and every pay phone in the store was covered. No one was found. Somehow, the caller had managed to escape through the basement employee entrance/exit—a door used only by employees and their relatives. This caused Roy Brown to think the caller may be an employee and that he probably was using the basement pay phone. The pay phone in the basement was situated where the mirrors in front of it reflected a good view of the desk where Kendra worked. He could dial the number and watch her reaction as he talked to her. Roy Brown explained to Kendra that very often those kinds of perverts are harmless, getting their enjoyment out *of watching the terror* on the faces of their victims, rather than actually hurting them.

Nevertheless, the thought of all this made Kendra even more terrified. She was not one bit consoled or comforted by this revelation. She was glad when summer ended, and she was back in college. She could leave the job far behind, which is what she chose to do. She would just find a part-time job elsewhere.

Three

Fall came and Kenneth and Keith began to plan some quail hunting trips in order to get enough for a quail Thanksgiving dinner. Keith's family was finally situated in Oklahoma City at their new address and Keith was ready to begin his graduate work at Oklahoma University. Kendra was beginning her senior year and would graduate in the spring. It had been seven months since she saw Keith for the first time at the church get-together for college students. During those seven months, her love for him had grown more with each passing day. She didn't acknowledge any negative traits that he may have because his smile, his touch, and his tenderness melted away all memory of them.

Thanksgiving came and Nell and Kenneth invited the Kouch family to join them for a quail dinner. Seated around the table with its platters of the golden-fried birds, Kenneth gave thanks for all their blessings. When he said, "Amen," Keith squeezed Kendra's hand under the table, and leaning over whispered to her, "*If I did, you would...*"

Cal Kouch sat sternly watching everyone; just waiting for a chance to bark orders to anyone that he felt wasn't behaving according to his standards. An overbearing man with a mean spirit, Edwina tried to cover for him by being cheerful and upbeat.

The twins did not come; Kyle was out of the country doing his military duties, and Kayla and her husband were expecting their first child, so Kayla couldn't travel. Cal spent most of the time during the dinner lauding the accomplishments of Kyle. It was as though he had no other children. Edwina tried to fill in the gaps with stories of their other two children, but somehow Cal always managed to come back to Kyle. It was obvious that he was proud of *him*. It was an awkward evening for Kenneth and Nell and their children, but they were gracious and kind for the sake of Keith and Edwina.

When cold weather arrived in full swing, one evening Kenneth called his family together in front of the fireplace and said he had an announcement to make. Kendra came down the stairs, followed closely by her two little sisters and her brother. Her sisters, Annanell and Abigail, at ages nine and ten were just fifteen months apart and had always seemed like twins. They were outgoing little girls, full of mischief and fun. They were olive-skinned like their father, too, but with blue eyes like their mother. Their long black hair was silky straight and they wore it in braids most of the time. Any time they could pester Kendra was the time they had the most fun. They especially loved to hide behind the divan when Kendra and Keith were sitting there talking.

Kendra's brother, Sammy was twelve years old and the perfect age to be a pest, too. He looked more like his mother with his blue eyes and golden red hair. Even though his face was peppered with freckles, he never burned when he was in the sun. The amber-colored freckles just got bigger and wider until they all ran together like golden syrup runs over a pancake. A cute little boy and a natural comedian, he could make anybody laugh with his whimsical antics. The accordion pleated sliding door that divided the living room from the playroom was a favorite place for Sammy to taunt the sweethearts as they sat together in the living room.

Mimicking the people who operated the elevators in the downtown department stores, Sammy slid open the folding door and loudly proclaimed: "Going up; first floor, men's wear, shoes and cosmetics. Watch your step, please." And he closed the divider, pretending to close the "elevator" door. This was his way of spying on them.

One night after Keith said goodnight to Kendra at the door, Sammy called to her as she reached the top of the stairs. He had something very important to ask her, he said. When she opened the door to his room, he was sitting on the side of the bed looking very worried.

"What's the matter, Sammy?"

"I just want to know something, Sis. *Can you breathe when you kiss or do you have to hold your breath?*"

It was those kinds of things that endeared Kendra's little brother to her. He was totally charming and innocent, and while he often got on her nerves, she loved him very, very, much.

When Kenneth and Nell thought they could not have more children after Kendra's birth, they were completely surprised eight years later when Sammy was born.

Then, the two girls followed shortly afterwards giving them the family for which they had often prayed.

By now they were all gathered in the living room for Kenneth to make his announcement. As calm as he always was, he lit his pipe, stoked the fire, and leaning against the mantle, spoke in a quiet and humble way. "I have decided to purchase a television for our Christmas present to all of you," he said. "I got it today and it will be delivered tomorrow."

The three youngest children let out a whoop and jumped up squealing and running around the room! "Yippee!" they yelled, and Abigail did a cartwheel, right there in the living room. Annanell followed suit and, not being as agile as Abigail, bumped the divan and landed flat on her back. It did not faze her and she jumped up, grabbed Abigail's hands and they "stitch-starched" all around the room. Millie, purring her approval, ran circles around the girls, her short legs slipping on the waxed, hardwood floor.

Kendra smiled sweetly and said, "Thanks, Daddy. We'll enjoy that so much." Nell just smiled with her "knowing look" and her look of total approval.

The next day the Zenith television arrived. It was in a huge console cabinet and it had a round screen. They could get three channels and the black and white pictures were sometimes fuzzy, but sometimes they were good, too. The family's interest and enjoyment of this new invention was instantaneous.

Keith came over on Tuesday nights to watch *I Love Lucy* with Kendra. It was their favorite show. Kenneth and Nell liked *The Gary Moore Show,* especially when Carol

Burnett made an appearance. *The Ozzie and Harriet Show* was everybody's favorite.

Sammy liked *The Roy Rogers Show* and the girls liked *Howdy Doody*. It was an exciting time in the Tinker household.

In many ways, the family was never the same. TV shows were substituted for the evening games of Forty-Two they had shared, and the crossword puzzles were all but forgotten. The house was quieter as they sat watching the picture instead of talking to one another as they had always done.

The family devotionals that Kenneth always led just before bedtime were being scheduled later in order for everybody to "watch their programs." Sometimes when a program ended, everyone was "too tired" and wanted to go on to bed without doing the devotionals.

It was with sadness that it became obvious to Kenneth that to make this new invention "family friendly," he would have to adjust the family's viewing habits. He did not want television to take precedence over the most important aspect of their lives, causing them to lose touch with that aspect.

His greatest strength lay in his willingness to take up his rightful place as Spiritual leader of his family, and as such, his children and wife greatly respected him and looked to him for guidance. It was from his example that Kendra got her strong religious convictions, and the determination and strength to abide by them. Her mother always backed her father in all of his decisions, giving all of their children a strong sense of love and security.

Four

Late one evening, Kendra was studying for upcoming tests in her classes, as the first semester would soon be winding down. Millie sat perched on the desk beside her and the phone rang. When she answered, it was Keith.

"Kendra, may I come over? I need to come tonight."

"Of course."

"I'll be right there." His voice sounded urgent.

Sammy knocked on her door, and peeking in, said, "Ohhh, did I hear you talking to Keith?" Then, in his mocking, sing-songy voice sang "My sister's in looove," and Kendra closed the door in his face.

"Get lost, little brother," she said to him, as the door slammed shut.

Keith would be there soon, and she had to change clothes. She always liked to look her best for him. She opened her closet door, and scanning her wardrobe, decided on her brown, velvet dress with the ecru lace collar. Slipping into the dress, she zipped the back, fastened the collar, and placed her amber cameo at her throat. She brushed her golden-red hair up and clipped it with a brown taffeta bow. And none too soon because at that precise moment, the doorbell rang.

Nell went to the door. "Who can that be at this hour?" she asked as she opened the door. Keith was standing there with his cycle helmet in his hand.

"Oh, hello, Keith, please come in. What brings you here this time of evening? It's almost 10:00. And did I hear your motorcycle?"

"You sure did. My car battery was dead and I have to talk to Kendra, so I rode my cycle." His eyes glistened and sparkled with happiness. "It's very important."

"Keith, is that you?" Kendra called from upstairs. And she swirled out of the room, quickly closing the door behind her. Millie barely escaped with her tail intact, but she managed to get through the door in time to follow Kendra down the stairs. It is a wonder the little cat didn't collapse from exhaustion. She was always running, trying to keep up with Kendra. The small white cotton ball seemed to think her main mission in life was to be wherever Kendra was.

"You look beautiful, Kendra," Keith said as she touched the last step of the stairs and blended into his arms. In a moment of shyness, he moved away, and placing his hands in his pockets, asked, "May we go somewhere we can be alone?"

Nell spoke up, "Keith, you two can use Kenneth's study; he's in the den preparing the evening devotional. We will gather in there when he's ready, so he won't be using the study."

She walked back into the sewing room to continue working on a sewing project for the girls. She was making angel costumes for Annanell and Abigail to wear in the Christmas Pageant at school. The teachers at school just couldn't pick *one* of the girls to be an angel and not the other one; it was always the same, if *one* was chosen for anything, so was the *other.* People just forgot they *weren't* twins.

Keith and Kendra slipped behind the closed door of her father's study and Keith took her by the hand and began to lead her to the leather couch. Millie sat outside the door and howled. Meeeowww—she wailed over and over loud and clear.

"That cat is a *pain*," Keith laughed. "She loves you as much as I do." As Kendra turned to let the kitten in, she thought, *did I hear that right? He loves me*? He said, *"If I did, you would"*...Does this mean that he *does,* and he means it's *me*?

Kendra opened the door, and Millie ran in, watching Kendra sit down on the divan. She promptly placed her plump body right down beside her, never taking those blue eyes off her, and purring all the while.

Kendra sat down, the rich brown, velvet dress spread around her in shimmering, soft folds. The lace collar and the cameo at her throat, combined with the cluster of curls clipped up in the brown taffeta bow, gave her the appearance of a Victorian lady of the past. She stroked Millie a second to let her know that she was aware of her purring presence, and turned to see Keith on his knees in front of her. He was holding a small box.

"Kendra, I love you. I want you to marry me. I can't wait for Christmas to tell you this." Kendra opened her mouth but before any words could come out, Keith continued.

"I tried *not to love you*—I didn't feel worthy of loving you, but *I knew if I ever did love anyone it would be you*—no one else. I do not deserve you, but I love you, oh, baby, how I love you. I haven't been able to eat or sleep or even think straight since I first came to the realization that there is *no* life for me without *you.*"

He began to fumble with the little box in his hands and he seemed to be all thumbs as he tried to open it.

Kendra felt her face flush with embarrassment, but the feeling in her heart and soul was so exuberant that she could hardly contain her excitement. *This beautiful, wonderful man loves me!* was all she kept thinking about. She wanted him to hold her, oh, how she wanted that, especially when he called her, "baby." When he finally got the box opened, he proudly put before Kendra a beautiful engagement ring.

"Merry Christmas, sweetheart!" He removed the ring from its velvet box and proudly held it before Kendra. It was the latest style of white gold and the large center stone was set in prongs up over the other stones alongside of it. Five stones ran down each side and ended in a "fishtail" design. Kendra thought it was the most beautiful ring she had ever seen because *Keith had chosen it!*

"Will you marry me?" he asked as he held the ring up in front of her.

"Oh, Keith, I love you with all of my heart. I would love to be your wife until such time as death separates us."

Keith stood up, and taking Kendra by the hands lifted her up next to him as he placed the ring on her finger.

Sliding his hands around her waist, he lifted her above his head, and slowly lowering her, he held her off the floor, kissing her tenderly. The kiss grew more passionate as he twirled her around in his arms until she felt dizzy and weak.

"Keith, put me down—please," she pleaded. "You must go ask Daddy about this. We can't forget his feelings in this matter, you know."

Keith eased her down and held her close for a few more minutes. Kendra felt that she had died and gone to Heaven. She had never been happier.

Hand in hand, they left the study and walked into the den. Kenneth was in the recliner with his Bible, note pad and pen in hand. He looked up when the two entered. He knew before a word was said what was happening.

"Kenneth, I love your daughter very much and I want her to be my wife."

Kenneth put aside his study papers and stared long and hard at the young couple before him, studying them with a careful, decisive eye. It seemed a long time, but at last, he spoke. "Do you both know the seriousness with which you should enter into this commitment? Do you know, Keith, that in our family, there is no such word as *divorce?* You must be sure you think this over carefully because what you decide is for *life*—you know that? You must love Kendra enough for it to last that long, and she must love you the same. *That is Biblical."*

"Yes sir, I understand that. You have my word on it. I will love her until death parts us—and even after that, sir, uh, *yes, sir!"*

"Kendra, do you love Keith in the same way that he says he loves *you?* Are you fully aware of the seriousness and the *responsibility you have before God to keep this commitment once you make it?"*

"Daddy, you know that I have loved Keith from the first time I ever saw him. I know you do, because I know Mother told you what I said about knowing the one I would marry when I met him."

"Then let's go tell your mother."

Nell was still at her sewing machine and the angel wings and glitter were all over her sewing table. She didn't have to ask what they wanted. She already knew.

She went straight over to Kendra and put her arms around her. Then she hugged Keith.

"Our daughter is a precious gem to us, Keith," she said as she moved away from him. Then turning back toward him, "We have brought her up to respect *us* and to respect *the Word of God.* We expect her to *respect you, too,* and for you to love her, to cherish her and to protect her all of her days. Anything short of that will cause us great sorrow and bring condemnation on you."

"Yes, Ma'am, I know that, Nell. That is what endears Kendra to me so much. You will never have to worry about her for one minute. I will cherish her until the day I die."

Kenneth walked over and put his arm around Nell.

"That is all we needed to hear," he said. "Now let's go tell the kids."

Abigail, Annanell, and Sammy had been instructed to turn off the television and study for their part in the evening family devotional, so they were sitting at the dining room table reading their verses when their parents and sister walked in with Keith.

"Okay, kids, you need to know that Keith here will be your brother-in-law very soon."

"That means your sister is going to be a *bride*," Nell added.

Again the squeals began. The two little girls began to chatter over which one would light the candles, and which one would be a bridesmaid. Sammy just turned up his nose, made an awful face and said, "Girls! Ugh! Keith, are you *crazy?*" and he walked out, shaking his head.

Kendra showed everyone her ring and the girls admired it, all the while giggling and whispering to one another.

"Will you stay and join in our devotional tonight, Keith? After all, you'll soon be a part of this family, too."

Keith stayed for the Tinker family devotional, sitting close to Kendra, both watching her ring sparkle, and both of them gazing at one another. They did not hear much of what was taking place, but Kenneth understood the distraction and made allowances for it this time.

It was 11:30 by the time the last prayer was said and the children were tucked into bed. Kenneth and Nell conveniently vanished upstairs to the master bedroom, leaving the end of the exciting evening to the lovebirds.

Keith held Kendra's face between his hands and moved his fingers into her hair. Unclipping the taffeta bow, he let it fall to the floor.

He was gentle and tender as he stroked her luxurious, long locks, then he pressed his mouth over hers; at first softly, then hard and long. She put her arms around his shoulders, and feeling very small indeed, disappeared into his strong, protective hug.

Then suddenly, with all the caution she could muster, Kendra pushed Keith away from her. "You must go now, Keith, it's best."

"I'll be back tomorrow and we can set a date. You be thinking about it, Kendra. I know that you will want a church wedding."

Then a quick kiss on the cheek, and opening the door, Keith was gone. Kendra listened as the sound of his motorcycle kicked up and she heard the three familiar turns of the throttle. *Buroomm, buroomm, buroomm* meaning *'I-love-you!'* and she waited by the door until the sound of his motorcycle faded into the night air.

Then Kendra closed the door and locked it. Turning out the light, she started up the stairs. But she could barely stand. She was weak and her legs were noodles. *It seems impossible to love someone so much*, she thought.

She sat right down on the bottom step and watched her ring sparkle as it picked up the light from the ever-glowing night light in the entryway. She turned her hand every way to reveal all of the different angles her ring would twinkle. All she could think of was Keith, their coming life together, and of how wonderful it would be to be his wife—forever.

As Kendra sat there, suddenly she felt a soft, timid nudge against her leg. It was Millie! Not to be forgotten in all of the excitement, she had been waiting patiently for Kendra under the stairwell, and now she came out to offer *her* congratulations, too!

"You precious kitten," she said, picking up the soft, round puff. "You know that you will come with me when I get married. I would never leave you, Millie."

And the kitten closed her eyes and with the top of her head, rubbed under Kendra's chin, all the while doing what she did best: purr.

Kendra stood up, draped Millie over her shoulder and ascended the stairs in a dream world. Once in her room and almost and in a state of unconsciousness, she slipped into her nightgown, brushed her hair back, splashed her face with cool water, brushed her teeth, and climbed between the sheets. She fluffed her pillow, turned it over on the "cold" side, and pulled up the edges around her face. Tomorrow they would meet together to set the date. She could hardly wait. Then, cradling the perpetually purring Millie in her arms, she sank into a sea of the sweetest dreams.

Five

Kendra was supposed to spend time studying for tests, and going downtown to look for another part-time job until she could graduate from college. But the events of the coming weeks took precedence over these plans. It was hard to concentrate on the tests she would be taking since Keith was coming over as soon as she got home.

He was right on time. He drove up just as Kendra was getting out of her car.

"Hi, beautiful!" he exclaimed, getting out of his car. "How is my Mrs. Today?" And his hug was so tight that he lifted her right off the ground.

"Keith!" Kendra exclaimed. "The neighbors—what will they *think*?"

"They'll just think I love my woman—my wife-to-be, that's all," he said grinning.

"Well, you know what Mother always says, 'Don't kiss in front of the garden gate; love may be blind, but the neighbors ain't!'" And she blushed and cupped her hands over her mouth, muffling a shy giggle.

"Come on, let's go downtown and look at the Christmas lights, and we can walk down Main Street and talk—bundle up really well even though we'll be keeping each other warm, too."

Keith parked the car at a meter on Main Street, and the two got out and began to walk. Christmas shoppers were out in full force and Christmas carols over loud speakers echoed all through the downtown area. Lights were ablaze and the atmosphere was one of happiness and cheer. Especially was that true in the hearts of the two sweethearts as they strolled the streets, talking of their wedding plans.

"Kendra, why don't we set the date the last of January, between semesters when you will have a few extra days? I will have extra days from O.U. also, and winter is a good season for a honeymoon, don't you think?"

"This January? You mean next month?" Kendra asked shocked.

"And just why not?" Keith asked.

"Well, it just seems *so quick*—will I have time to plan the wedding I've always *dreamed of?"*

"You can do it, Kendra. I'm anxious to begin our life together—it can't happen *too quickly for me*!"

"I'm anxious, too, Keith. But I was thinking of a spring wedding after I graduate and get resumes sent out. I would like to have a job possibility on the horizon first. You will not be quite finished with your graduate work, and I would need to have a good job."

Keith suddenly stopped in front of J. C. Penney's, turned and took Kendra by the shoulders. Looking directly into her face, the brown eyes clouded and deepening to the now familiar darkness, he tightened his grip on her so that she cried out in pain.

"Keith, you're hurting me," she cried, her eyes beginning to tear.

"Do you think that I cannot support a wife? Do you think I am not good enough to take care of you?" He raised his voice and clenched his teeth. Passersby were beginning to look. Kendra was embarrassed.

"Keith, people are looking at us. Please calm down. I know you're good enough. I just wanted you to finish school and I wanted to be able to help pay some of the bills until you did. That's all."

Keith released the grip he had on Kendra, the darkness of his eyes subsiding as he pulled her close.

"Okay, sweetheart, whatever you want to do is fine with me," he said as the soft, warm brown eyes returned to haunt her with their gentleness. "So what about the last of May? You should have some offers by then."

"A May wedding would be perfect," Kendra replied and the last few moments, like a vapor, vanished from her mind.

"Then it's all set, Kendra. Let's dash in here for some hot cocoa and warm up a bit before walking back to the car." And they walked into the Main Street Coffee Shop and sat down on a counter stool. Kendra ordered her favorite, hot chocolate with a scoop of vanilla ice cream in it, and Keith got just plain cocoa with cookies.

"Do you have a pocket calendar?" he asked.

"Yes, I do—here in my purse." Kendra took out her daily planner and calendar.

"Let's see, Kendra. Look at May and see what you think. How about a Saturday night?"

"Okay, Saturday, May twenty-fifth looks perfect. What time?"

Keith didn't know that Kendra had already set this date in her mind. She had already done the necessary calculating and had decided upon this date long ago when she first knew it was Keith she wanted to marry.

"Well, I know that you want a formal wedding so let's go for about 8:00 p.m." and he grinned that adorable grin that could melt Kendra into a warm puddle.

"All right! I will begin the planning, Keith. I already know every way I want it to be. I have known and dreamed of my wedding since I was a little girl. It will have to be in blue."

They finished their cocoa and ventured back out into the cold.

"Where do you plan to apply for your part-time job this time, Kendra?" Keith asked as they began walking back toward the car. "I know you want to get as far away as you can from Brown's and that caller you had."

"I'm going to apply at Kerr's," she said. "They have an excellent employee discount policy and I can buy my wedding things there with that discount."

"I'm sure your old man will help you; he has *scads* of money."

Suddenly and as a complete surprise to Keith, Kendra stopped and turned to him, her eyes flashing with anger.

"Never refer to my father as 'your old man'—and I mean *never!* He is *my father* and I respect him and *you will, too*, or I *won't* become Mrs. Keith Kouch!" And she turned from Keith and began to stomp down the sidewalk away from him as fast as she could go.

Keith had never before seen Kendra express any anger; indeed, he had often wondered if there was *anything* that *could* upset her.

Running after her, he caught up with her and apologized.

"Hey, little girl, I'm sorry! I admire your dad. I just made a thoughtless remark." And he took her in his arms.

Something about the way he said, "Hey, little girl," gave Kendra a chill. But as always, the strong arms and gentle touch saturated Kendra's loving heart, and she once again succumbed to his sheltering hug.

"Okay, Keith—it's just that my parents mean the world to me. They've sacrificed everything so I could have the best of all the things I love. They've given me music lessons from an early age because they know how much I love it. They've always been there for me, and have always given my siblings and me a loving, secure home. The Bible has always been our guide, and they have made sure that we know that. I can't let *you* or *anyone else* degrade that image—*ever.* "

Arms around each other, the two walked back to the car. The meter had expired and a ticket was stuck under the windshield wiper. Keith muttered as he put it in his pocket.

"Oh, well, we can put this as a keepsake in our family scrapbook. It may be fun to reflect on it someday." And they started back home. Kendra couldn't wait to tell her parents the date they had set.

At the door, Keith gathered Kendra's fur lined hood up over her hair, and clasping it by its edges, he pulled her close, kissed her lips, hard and long. Moving his kiss onto her cheeks and neck, he murmured, "I love you, Kendra; you will never know how much."

Kendra eased herself away, and cupped his face in her hands, stroking his cheeks lightly with the back of her hand.

"I love you, too Keith—and I always will. Good night." And she turned and went inside.

Keith sat in his car a few moments before starting the engine, then eased the car out the drive and onto the street.

Nell and Kenneth were both happy for Kendra. Annanell and Abigail were ecstatic and did what they always did best: squeal. Sammy was *not impressed.*

"Probably have to wear a stupid *monkey suit,*" he grumbled.

"That's right, Sammy," Kendra replied. "This wedding will be a *family affair.* Annanell and Abigail, you will *both* be bridesmaids. And Sammy, you will be an usher and you *will wear a 'monkey suit'* because it is going to be formal, so get used to the idea, little brother." And she scrubbed his head, mussing his waxed flat-top, causing it to wilt a bit.

"Ah, stop it, Sis," he complained.

"May twenty-fifth—ta-da-ta-da, ummmm, I will give My Love, my love, oh how happy we will be...." Kendra sang as she pulled out the piano bench, sat down, and began to compose her own wedding song. Of course, Millie hopped right up there beside her on the bench, her eyes wide with wonderment, the pupils dilated with excitement.

This would be the song she would sing directly *to* Keith face to face before the altar. She would look directly into those warm brown eyes, and he would *feel* every word as she sang it to him. Moving her fingers around over the keys, Kendra had already put the words in her mind; all she needed to do now was create the tune:

"I give you my love, My Love, for as long as I live,
It is everything for you that I have to give.
I love you, Keith, deeper far than any sea,
I'll be your wife—Through all eternity.
You are my strength, my armor, and my heart.
With you, I am whole; without you, a part.
So now I give you my love,
      My Love, forever and a day,
And I will truly begin to live
      this twenty-fifth day of May!"

"Well, Millie, what do you think?" she asked, turning to the inquisitive kitten beside her. "I think it needs work, but for now, I like it."

Millie looked intently at Kendra as she talked, and when she finished, the kitten took her little walk on the keys and jumped down, her tail in its questioning mode; straight up with a curved hook on the end like a question mark.

"Beautiful!" Nell called from the kitchen where the good smells of Christmas were beginning to permeate the house. "That's going to be perfect for the wedding!" Semester finals over, Kendra could now look forward to Christmas break and she planned to use the time wisely. She would go apply for the part-time job at Kerr's and the very first thing she would do, if hired, would be to visit their Bridal Shop on the third floor.

Six

Kendra chose one of her nicest dresses to go apply for the Kerr's position. It was a sky-blue, wool sheath dress with long sleeves and a blue satin cummerbund. She wore her blue spring-o-lators with the double strap on each toe. She brushed her hair, letting it fall into its natural curls, but sweeping a few of them up on one side with a blue moonstone Monet barrette. For finishing touches, she added her blue moonstone earrings.

When Kendra walked into the personnel office of Kerr's Department Store, she made quite an impression on the personnel manager. She was a picture of dignity, class, and poise, making her a very credible candidate for the job.

She handed Mr. Fuller the application and he asked her to sit down. He put on his glasses, and as he read, the glasses kept sliding down his nose. He pushed them back up each time, leaned over the desk, scrutinized the young lady in front of him, then returned to eyeing the paper. Kendra's heart was pounding. What *was* he thinking?

"So you left your last employer because you were getting obscene calls?"

"Yes, it was interfering with my job performance. You may check my references and also you may speak with my former employer if you wish."

"Ah, yes, I intend to do just that," he replied as he picked up the second sheet of the application.

Silence. Kendra thought the silence embarrassing. She felt like she ought to say something. But she remained quiet and tried to appear poised and self-confident.

At long last, he spoke.

"So did you ever find out who was making the calls?"

"No sir, we never did find out. Roy Brown, the House Detective suspected an employee, but never could prove it." Kendra was breathless.

"I know Roy Brown. He's a friend of mine. Often works the House detective position over here, too. I think he spends a few days at one store and a few with us, rotating the days each week. I can speak to him about this."

"I have put his name down for a reference, and also Judy McClure's name, who hired me. Feel free to contact them both."

Mr. Fuller stood up, indicating he was through with her so she stood also. Extending his hand, Kendra took it.

"You'll be hearing from me in a few days, Kendra. Goodbye."

"Thank you, Mr. Fuller." And Kendra gathered her coat onto her arm, and walked out.

"Well, Kendra, how do you think the interview went today?" Nell asked her as she came in the door.

"I don't know for sure, Mom. He just read and re-read everything and didn't say much. I'm afraid the calls are going to keep me from being considered, though. He seemed more interested in them than in any qualifications I have. That is all he talked about."

"Well, don't worry, honey. If you are meant to work there, then you'll have the opportunity. And just remember it's only for a short while. I'm sure that with your musical talents, the offers will come in just as soon as you graduate and you won't need that job anyway."

The next few days, Kendra practiced her piano with more fervor than ever. She learned new pieces that she perfected after only a few tries.

There was absolutely nothing Kendra couldn't play. Her talents were unending in the musical field. Kenneth and Nell thought she should pursue higher goals than just to *teach* music. She could compose lyrics and music with just the touch of the ivory, and she made it all *look* so simple.

Her countenance, as she played, was radiant. She appeared to be in another world when her fingers brushed across the piano keys, seeming to barely touch them, and she looked like an angel. When she sang, she *sounded* like one, too.

One afternoon, Kendra left her piano to answer the phone.

"May I speak with Kendra Tinker?" the voice asked.

"This is Kendra."

"Kendra, this is Jerry Fuller at Kerr's. I need to speak with you concerning your application. Could you possibly come back down to my office immediately?"

"I will be there in thirty minutes, Mr. Fuller." And she hung up the phone.

"Mom!" she called. "I have to go back to see Mr. Fuller. I will be back in awhile!"

She quickly changed her clothes and ran out to her car. She was at his office door within thirty minutes of his call just as she said she would be.

"Come in, Kendra and have a seat."

Kendra's heart was racing. What was he going to tell her?

"Kendra, we have decided to hire you, but not for the job as advertised."

Kendra's heart sank. She just knew she was going to have to take a job for which she was not trained. She braced herself for what she thought was inevitable.

"As you may not know, Kendra, the fifteenth floor of our store is a musical studio, school, and store. Kind of a 'store-within-a store-school.'"

No, Kendra was not aware that the top story of the Kerr building was a musical studio, school, and store. A store for the very rich, she had always felt brave to just go inside the first floor where the jewelry was. She had seen the ads for the Bridal Service on the third floor but somehow had never known about the exclusive, private music store on the fifteenth floor.

Mr. Fuller continued. "It's a very large section of the company and the entire floor is made up of our musical department. There is an area for private music lessons, a studio for recording, a dance floor for ballet, and an area where all instruments are for sale. This floor is not advertised to the public because it serves an exclusive clientele. A family who chooses to remain anonymous purchased it through our company in memory of a daughter who loved to play the piano. They wanted to provide every advantage for gifted children to develop their talents."

Mr. Fuller continued, "Most people who enroll in it are those who are unusually gifted in music. We service many talented students, not only in Oklahoma City, but we have some who come from abroad to study with us. Some of the school's graduates go on to Broadway and the big time."

"Oh, I wasn't aware of such a facility at Kerr's," Kendra replied.

"Well, my dear," Mr. Fuller replied, "this is where you come in."

Kendra's mind escalated. Where was this going? What would she say?

"I have checked all of your references, and even checked with OCU; they all say the same thing. For years, now, we have had difficulty finding a teacher/manager/buyer for this area of our store. If we find one qualified as a teacher, her manager skills are not good. If we find a good manager possibility, then the musical skills are lacking, and so on. But in you, we found *all three*!

"We are very excited to offer you this position and we hope that when you graduate, you will stay with us. It will pay you well, and you will have the opportunity to go to New York with graduates and tutor and train them there. You may even eventually find a spot for *your* talents *there, too.* It could open up all kinds of possibilities for your future, Kendra. What do you say?"

Kendra was stunned with disbelief. The words in her heart just stuck there for a long time before she could say anything.

"Oh, Mr. Fuller," she finally managed to say. "I would love it. I can teach music all I want to?"

"Yes, you can, plus you can buy the instruments you think we need, and manage the school all at the same time. We will start you part-time and when you finish college come May, you'll be ready for full-time work and will know the school by heart. Your job with us will be secure because the school is set up to never run out of money. You will be able to stay as long as you wish and your salary will be more than adequate. Shall be begin next Monday?"

"That will be perfect!" Kendra exclaimed. "You know that I'll be getting married on May twenty-fifth, so this will work out just perfect! Oh, Mr. Fuller, thank you so much!"

"Believe me, Kendra, it is *our pleasure.* After speaking with the OCU counselors, the president—all of them—we know that we have the cream of the crop. So *thank you*!" And he stood up.

Kendra knew it was time to go.

"I will be here on Monday afternoon—*count on it!"*

And she felt that she *literally floated* out the door.

Seven

Kenneth and Nell couldn't have been happier for Kendra. A blessed child, for whom they had prayed, they considered her a gift from God. Nell had suffered a difficult pregnancy and was told there was a possibility that her baby would be born with multiple handicaps.

But when Kendra was born, she was blessed with beauty as well as good health, and this unexpected realization put Kenneth and Nell on their knees in thanksgiving. Then, to learn of her many talents were just more blessings than they could count. They determined to always let Kendra know what a lovely blessing she was. And through it all, Kendra remained unselfish and unspoiled, adding to her inner beauty.

Kendra could hardly wait to tell Keith her news. Nell had always taught her daughters not to call boys, so even though she and Keith were engaged, it was still something very hard for Kendra to do.

"Well, we *are* getting married," she whispered to herself as she dialed Keith's number.

She was so excited as she talked to Keith that she was breathless as she explained everything that happened in the interview.

"I'm happy for you—for us," Keith replied.

But something in the tone of his voice worried Kendra. He sounded a little jealous—*no!* Surely she was imagining such a thing. *Keith loved her*—he wouldn't be jealous of *her*—of *their*—good fortune. And she hung up the phone, determined not to think on it at all.

Monday morning seemed slow in coming for Kendra. She could hardly wait. Up bright and early, she accidentally nudged Millie out of a deep sleep, momentarily forgetting the kitten was beside her. Millie unwound herself in a wide stretch on the satin comforter, her mouth opening wide in a yawn. She shook herself and jumped off the bed, all the while watching Kendra.

"My first day, Millie," she said. "I'm starting my new job. Wish me luck," and she tickled the bright-eyed kitten under its chin.

She dressed quickly but took extra time putting on her make up and fixing her hair. Millie sat on the vanity, eyes glued to the mirror, looking with affection at her mistress.

"Let's go eat breakfast, Millie," she said and the two hurried out and down the stairs.

Nell had already put breakfast on the table.

"Kendra, you are already dressed for work? You are part-time; why are you going in so early? You don't have to be there until 1:00."

"Oh, Mom, I want to get there early enough to go to the third floor Bridal Salon. I want to go through catalogues and look at all the dresses in order to choose what I want. I want the prettiest, fluffiest, laciest white dress I can find," she said, her eyes sparkling with the dreams she was seeing in her mind.

Kenneth and Nell always taught their daughters that when they got married, they could wear white only if they have earned the right to do so. They would never allow marriage to become a mockery by having a daughter wear white who was unworthy to wear it.

They made sure that the girls knew white symbolizes purity, and they told them they could have the wedding of their dreams if they stayed true to that symbolism.

It's going to be a pleasure to give this girl the wedding she has dreamed of since she was a child, Nell thought, as Kendra's excitement kept bubbling over like a boiling pot of water.

"And Mom, I also want to have time to go up to the fifteenth floor and get a feel of the area and what I'll be doing before 1:00 comes."

The Oklahoma wind was whistling around the house as Kendra shut the door and hurried out to the garage. Millie ran behind her and jumped onto the windowsill, parting the curtains, watching her best friend leave.

Kendra glanced back to see the little white face steadfastly pressed against the window, small bursts of fog hitting the glass with each puff of breath against it.

The day was becoming dreary and blustery outside. The weatherman said there was an eighty percent chance of a white Christmas, and the sky was overcast with heavy, gray clouds, indicating that he may be right.

Kendra pulled her hood up over her head, slipped on her mittens and tightened her belt around her coat. The garage door was frozen and hard to lift, but finally inside, she let the car warm up a bit before finally backing out and driving away.

When she stepped inside Kerr's, she was impressed with all of the holiday decorations. It was a beautiful wonderland of lights, trees, holly, and garland. She walked over to the elevator. She knew that since the elevator operator stopped at every floor, the wait might be longer than she wanted it to be. She seriously considered walking the stairs, but decided against it since she was in her high-heeled shoes.

Finally, the "ping" sound and the cover door of the elevator opened. The operator, with a thick protective glove on one hand, used it to pull back the second door, a heavy iron lattice door with a bulky latch.

"Going up. Please watch your step," she called out politely to all of the waiting patrons as they filed into her car. Then she closed first one door, then the other, latching it securely before turning the cylinder that propelled the elevator to the next floor.

There were so many people out shopping already and the store had barely opened. It seemed to take forever to get to the third floor. Kendra was anxious.

"Mezzanine. Customer Service, Layaway, Business Office, and Public Restrooms. Watch your step, please," the operator repeated as the elevator stopped, and she opened the doors again. *Having to stop on the Mezzanine floor was causing the assent to be even slower,* Kendra thought. *And what a boring job she has. I don't envy her saying the same things hour after hour. There was one thing good about it, though; she had a little stool over in the corner of the elevator where she could sit down some of the time.*

Finally, the announcement came: "Third floor, Bridal Salon. Watch your step."

The doors opened and Kendra was the only one to get off at that stop. She was glad.

As she looked over the area, her eyes lit up in anticipation. Everything was white and lacy—and beautiful! She didn't know where to begin. It was so much to take in all at once. When she found the dress of her dreams, she would know it!

A bridal consultant walked over to Kendra and asked to help her. She handed Kendra a catalogue to look through and informed her that the dresses were behind locked doors unless she selected a "special order" one. She told her if there was one she wanted to try on to let her know.

Kendra sat down on the divan in the area for browsing and began to look through books. It didn't take her long to locate exactly what she was wanted. Her vision was a gown of lace or net over satin, a high neck, puffed sleeves, and satin trim. She wanted to wear a hoop under it and wanted it to be as full as Scarlet O'Hara's dresses were in *Gone with the Wind.*

"I'd like to try on this one," she told the consultant, and she pointed to a dress on a page all by itself where she could plainly see all of the detail on the bodice and skirt.

"Oh, you'll love that one, my dear," she said. "We just got it in but it only comes in sizes six and eight. It's a long version of the dress Grace Kelly wore in the movie, *High Society* with Bing Crosby. What size do you need?"

"I need a size six," Kendra replied.

59

The lady disappeared behind the doors and returned carrying a long gown in a plastic bag.

She ushered Kendra to the fitting room where all the walls were covered with mirrors, allowing a buyer to see from every angle. With her clipboard in hand, the Bridal Consultant began to question Kendra about all of her plans.

"I begin work today on the fifteenth floor music school and I wanted to come here first before I clock in at 1:00," Kendra explained.

"My name is Betty, and I want to help you in every way I can. We offer complete bridal assistance, from flowers to reception, to invitations; everything you need is all right here on this floor. And you will be able, as an employee, to buy everything with a twenty-five percent discount. Now let me go get you the necessary foundation, hoop and crinoline so that you may see how this dress will look."

Kendra removed the gown from its bag and gasped at its beauty. There was no need to look further. This was *it!* It was just as she had dreamed it would be. The net circular skirt, embroidered with tiny flowers, floated over two layers of soft tulle, covering heavy white satin. The puffed sleeves had ten covered buttons fastened with satin loops running up the wrist to the elbow, and the back had eighty-five covered buttons fastened with satin loops. The satin piping around the waist dipped into a point in the front, and the stand-up collar was edged in satin.

Betty came back into the fitting room carrying a merry widow, crinoline, and hoop. She spread the hoop to its maximum and Kendra slipped into it, then tossed the crinoline over her head and let it billow down over the hoop. She hooked the merry widow, in place, and Betty assisted her in getting the dress on over her head. She fluffed the dress out evenly all around, and buttoned all the buttons for her. Then she stood back for a full view from all angles.

"Magnificent!" Betty exclaimed. Kendra couldn't believe her eyes. The dress' skirt was so full she wondered if it would fit down the church aisle. But she felt like a princess! Betty interrupted her thoughts.

"Kendra, you are going to want this to fit tighter in the waist so that the beauty of the billowing skirt can be appreciated."

She took a tape measure and measured Kendra's waist.

"Honey, this size six is going to have to be taken up a little bit. Your waist is twenty-one inches, and the dress is twenty-three inches. We want a snug fit, and it doesn't come in a size smaller than this."

Betty wrote down all of the measurements and packed the dress back into its bag. Kendra went to look for a headpiece.

She selected a tiara type crown with an elbow-length veil. The crown stood up about four inches, and the loops and hearts were covered with rhinestones and iridescent pearls. The soft tulle she selected for the veil would be attached to the crown later.

Betty pinned the areas that needed altering and wrote down all that Kendra told her. The wedding would be all blue, Kendra's favorite color, and she would look another day for just the right dresses for her bridesmaids. She looked at her watch: It was 12:00 and she had just one hour to go upstairs and look over the place where she would soon be working.

She left the dress to be altered, placed it in layaway and went back out to the elevators, elated that she had so easily found her dream gown. She was walking on the clouds as she thought about showing it to everybody at home. She could hardly wait!

Kendra thought the elevator was slow getting to the *third* floor; she knew it would *never* get to the *fifteenth*.

Finally, she stepped from the elevator into what seemed to her to be another world. It was a wonderful studio! There was so much to see that she wondered if she could possibly see all of it in one day.

She stopped by the receptionist's desk to let her know she was there, and the receptionist called Mr. Fuller. He was there in a matter of minutes.

"Hello, there, Kendra. Ready to begin?"

"I sure am, Mr. Fuller."

"Then let's get busy."

All too soon 5:30 rolled around and the day ended for Kendra's first day on her new job. There was so much to learn and so much to do that she felt overwhelmed, but she knew she was going to love it!

She met her students and their parents and began compiling the records on each one, learning more about them all the time. Sarah was a shy little girl, but her musical ability was just phenomenal, and Kendra was anxious to get her started. There were five other students, but not all played the piano. Sarah did, as well as two other little girls. The others were interested in ballet, vocal, or other instruments. Kendra would be qualified to teach everything they offered when she graduated in May. And with these thoughts, she hurried out of the store.

Walking to the parking garage, she was barely able to withstand the wind. It had picked up considerably, and she was very cold. By the time she reached her car, a light mist and snow were beginning to fall.

She warmed the car a little, but not too long, for she was anxious to get home and tell everyone about her day.

She pulled into the drive just as the snow began to fall hard and fast. She got out and opened the garage door, got back into the car, and drove it in. She stomped the snow off her boots and came in through the back door, and into the kitchen. Millie bounced in, making her chirping noises when she saw her.

Nell had hot stew and cornbread ready on the stove, and the family was just waiting for Kendra to get home so they could eat supper.

"Hurry, Kendra, and come sit down and tell us about your day."

Annanell, Abigail, and Sammy sat motionless at the table for a change; all were eager to learn what Kendra would say.

Then all began to chatter at once, everybody except Sammy, who was making his usual nausea sounds that he made when "girl things" were discussed.

Nell brought in the huge pot of stew, the pan of cornbread, then filled the glasses with iced tea. Then she seated herself next to Kenneth.

"Okay, everybody, let's give Kendra time to sit down and catch her breath," Kenneth said, interrupting the chatter.

"Oh, Daddy, I had the most wonderful day—you just can't imagine. I don't know where to start! I think I'll start with my dress..." and she took her place beside the girls.

"You got your wedding dress?" Abigail and Annanell asked simultaneously, their eyes wide with excitement.

"*Yes*!" Kendra glowed with happiness.

"Daddy, you and Mom went to see the picture show, *High Society*, didn't you?

"Yes, just a week or so ago. Why?"

"My gown is a copy of the wedding dress Grace Kelly wears in that show, except mine is the floor length version while hers is ballerina length. Oh, it is sooooo pretty," and she clasped her hands together and propped her elbows on the table.

"The stew is getting cold, so let's give thanks and we can talk as we eat," Kenneth reminded them.

All six of them joined hands around the round table and Kenneth gave thanks for the food, his family, and his daughter's happiness.

Now it was Kendra's turn. Everyone listened, spellbound, as she told of the day and selecting her wedding gown. Just as supper was almost finished, the phone rang.

"I'll get it!" Sammy interrupted. "I'm tired of this ol' girl-stuff talk, anyway!" And he ran in the kitchen to answer the phone.

"Kendra! It's for you—it's Keitheeeeeeee smack, smack, smack.... Yuck!"

Kendra got up from the table and went in the kitchen.

"Hello, Keith, guess what? I got my dress today!" Kendra said as she took the phone from Sammy's hand. Then cupping her hand over the receiver, she said,

"Honestly, Sammy, you're a mess—now go get lost!"

Sammy shrugged his shoulders and sauntered out the door, smirking.

"That's great, sweetheart," Keith replied. "I won't ask you to describe it; it's bad luck; besides, I want to be surprised. Just wish it wasn't five months away!"

Kendra smiled to herself and Keith continued.

"My folks are back from Kayla's house. Her baby was a girl and they named her Wendy. They had a wonderful time. This is their first grandchild, you know. They are glad to be back home and they want you to come over tonight. They want us to go over all the plans we've made. They also want to see the ring *on your finger*! They said they wouldn't believe it until they could *see* it! Could you come over in an hour or so?"

"I'll be over right after supper!"

"Okay, hon, I will see you then."

Kendra went back into the dining room and sat back down to finish her supper. It was a little difficult to concentrate on anything but all of the things that happened that day. It was one of the most wonderful days of her life.

"Mom, I am going to run over to Keith's house for a while. Cal and Edwina want to see my ring and to hear about all of our plans. They've missed all of the excitement *here* because of the excitement in *Arkansas*. They're anxious to catch up. I won't be gone long."

When Kendra rang the Kouches' doorbell, Keith appeared almost instantly. He had been watching out the window for her arrival. He took her coat, lovingly placed his arm around her shoulders, and hugged her. Kendra felt loved and a feeling of warmth engulfed her.

Edwina came from the kitchen and greeted her graciously, beaming all the while. "Let me see your ring finger," she asked, and Kendra held out her hand.

"Oh, Kendra, that's so beautiful, and you can't know how pleased we are to know that you are going to be our second daughter. When Keith called us at Kayla's house with the news, we felt it was every bit as exciting as seeing our first grandchild. Come on in the living room and sit down."

Keith followed Kendra and his mother to the living room and he and Kendra sat down beside one another on the divan. Edwina sat across from them in the armchair.

Cal, with his intimidating air of superiority strolled in, looking stern and solemn. He walked over to Kendra, bent down, took her hand in his and eyed the ring thoroughly, saying nothing but, "Uh-huh—hummmmm—okay." Then he took a seat in the recliner in front of the fireplace.

Kendra felt a bit nervous as she watched him sit down, scoot all the way back in the chair, and sit as straight as a board, feet neatly side by side, and hands folded in his lap.

"All right, now let's hear it, tell me what your plans are." His moustache twitched as he spoke.

"Well—" Kendra and Keith began both at the same time. They laughed and Keith said, "Go ahead, Kendra, you tell Dad and Mom about your job, your dress, and everything."

As Kendra spoke, Cal's response was cold and unresponsive. But Edwina could not remain still.

Everything she heard Kendra say, she interspersed with an excited phrase. She literally bounced in her chair listening to Kendra speak.

"Wonderful! How exciting! I am *so* happy!" over and over, the lady said, bubbling with as much enthusiasm as Kendra.

Then Keith spoke.

"Mom, Dad, I love Kendra more than I have ever loved anyone. She is the girl I have picked as my wife for the rest of my life. You both will love her as I do, and you will see what a wise choice I have made. We're going to have a church wedding on Saturday, May twenty-fifth and we plan to make it a *family affair.*"

Edwina excused herself to go make some coffee and left the two young people with Cal. The silence was embarrassing to Kendra, and Keith seemed nervous as Cal just sat there, staring at them, hard and long.

It was a relief when Edwina came back into the room. Just coming in the door, the tension was eased. She was like a slice of sunshine when she entered a room.

"Come, my dear," she said to Kendra. "I want to speak with you in the kitchen."

Kendra got up and obediently followed her future mother-in-law.

"Kendra, we are happy that Keith has found someone like you—we believe that he *can* and *will* stay married to someone with your personality. You are *good* for him and you make him a *better person.* Just remember, no matter what happens, Keith *loves you.* There may be times that you do not believe this, but don't get discouraged; you must always remember that underneath it all, his love is *deep and real.* I have never seen him like this before—he is different when you are with him, and that's *good*!"

She hugged Kendra and the two women went back into the living room. Cal stood when they walked in and Keith was looking rather sheepish.

"I think I better go now, Keith."

"I'll walk you to your car."

Keith got her coat out of the hall closet, put it around her shoulders, and the two walked outside.

"Keith, what did your dad say? Does he approve?"

"Yes, he approves, Kendra. He just has a very difficult time showing emotions. Mother understands him and says that he is thrilled with my choice. He just can't express it to *us*. I'm sorry."

Keith opened the car door for Kendra, but before she could get in, he pulled her close and kissed her goodnight.

She got in her car and drove away, contemplating the evening in a thoughtful, questioning way. By the time she reached her house, she had convinced herself that everything was all right, and would *always be all right.*

Eight

In the days to follow, Kendra fell more and more in love with her new job. Sarah, even with her handicap, was turning out to be a child prodigy and Kendra took advantage of every opportunity to see that the little girl's talents were utilized to the fullest. She loved her job so much she could hardly wait for it to become full-time. Watching her students grow with improvement became her first priority and every step taken toward success was a step toward success for Kendra. Life for her was so *gooood,* and she had never been happier.

Christmas Eve, Keith came by to get Kendra, inviting her to go look at the lights in North Oklahoma City. He also told her he had a gift for her. Kendra had something for him, too, but she didn't tell him right away.

"But Keith, my ring was my gift. I hope you didn't get something else."

They drove around through all the neighborhoods of Nichols Hills admiring the beautiful, decorated homes, then Keith stopped the car. He reached over and opened the glove compartment, took out a small box and handed it to Kendra.

Very carefully, Kendra opened the box. Inside was a large gold locket on a gold box chain. Engraved on the back were the words:

"Kendra, *'If I did, you would,'* is now *'I do and you are*!' All my love, Keith."

Kendra looked up at him and threw her arms around his neck.

"Oh, Keith, it is beautiful! I will wear it with my gown for 'something new.' Thank you so much—I am so proud of it!" And she giggled until Keith was puzzled.

Keith placed his hands on her neck and tilted her chin up and kissed her with the affection that she had come to expect.

"I will always love you, my Kendra." He started the car and they began their trip home.

"Keith, I have a gift for you, too." Kendra said, her eyes shining, the giggling beginning again.

She reached down in her pocket, took out a box and gave it to Keith. He stopped the car again and opened it. Both began to laugh. What a coincidence their gifts were!

Nestled inside the box was a gold ID bracelet. On one side it said "Keith Kouch," and engraved on the other side was:

"To Keith with all my love, Kendra. *I do, and you are.*"

They grabbed each other and hugged and kissed and laughed.

Their Christmas Eve together came to an end when Keith walked Kendra to the door. Both would be spending Christmas Day with their own families. Keith's sister and her husband, together with their new baby, and his brother, home from overseas, would get to be there. And of course, Kendra's family would all be together, so it was with a great reluctance that they said goodnight. It was getting harder and harder to say goodbye. They both looked forward to May when they wouldn't have to be apart anymore.

Christmas morning at the Tinker home began with a hot breakfast. Nell started a fire in the fireplace and put on Christmas music, as the house was warm and cozy and alive with the good sounds and smells of Christmas.

Everybody was going to open presents after breakfast, so Kenneth reminded them that they had already gotten their gift from him when he gave them the television. And he chuckled with a twinkle in his eyes.

The girls in their flannel granny gowns, Sammy in his Superman pajamas and Kendra in her thick, warm, chenille robe came bopping down the stairs with Millie close behind trying to keep up.

Nell had gotten up early and put the turkey on to roast for Christmas dinner and its smell was already filling the house with its mouth-watering aroma.

She even had the dining room table all set complete with the Christmas centerpiece the girls made. The family gathered around the tree after the breakfast dishes were done.

"Whose turn is it to be the Elf this year and pass out the presents?" Sammy asked.

"*You* get to do it this year, little man," Kendra answered.

"Sounds good to *me*," Sammy replied, taking his seat beside the tree branches to begin sorting out the packages. In a big hurry, he picked out all the ones with his name written on the tag, and stacked them in a neat pile beside him. Then one by one, he began to call out the names.

"Kendra, you're first," he said, handing her a package with silver and blue wrappings and trim.

"Let's all unwrap one at a time," Nell said, "then, we can see what everybody gets." But Sammy wanted to tear into all of his right that minute. Being outnumbered, he had to wait, and he stuck out his lip in a mock pout.

Millie crawled up right smack dab into the middle of Kendra's lap, turned around a few times and settled herself down with a ringside seat. Her eyes darted from package to package and she eyed the ribbons and tissue until she could no longer contain herself. Kendra tried hard to unwrap the package, but Millie kept batting at the bow, making it difficult.

"Behave, Millie, or I'll have to put you down."

Millie just looked up at her with question marks in her eyes. "Ribbons are just *made* for kittens, how could she 'behave?'" Nell asked.

Finally, Kendra got the paper off, revealing a box with a grosgrain ribbon hanging from it. She pulled up on it, and the tiny lid opened.

"Ohhh..." squealed Kendra. "This is beautiful! Look at this, Millie!"

The watch Kendra took out of the box had diamonds around the edge and in the center of the ceramic face of the watch, was a painting of Millie. Her father had taken a photo of Millie and had an artist paint it on the blue background, matching perfectly Millie's blue eyes. The narrow wristband was gold with tiny diamond chips covering it in a pave' setting. Kendra had never seen anything like it!

"Daddy! This is gorgeous! Thank you, thank you!" Kendra jumped up, spilling Millie off her lap, to give her father a kiss and a hug.

"That's from your mother and me," he said. "We know how much that little cat means to you, and we thought this was a good way to show it."

"Thanks, Mom!" and she hugged her mother. Nell beamed.

Sammy passed around the presents one by one and each person opened his special package.

There was a kit for Sammy, complete with everything he needed to build a go-cart; something he had wanted for a long, long time. The kit even included the flame stencil to paint on the side and he quickly named his Go-Cart-to-be, *Flying Flames*. Then he opened his other presents. One contained a helmet with the flames on the side, and another contained a baggy racing suit to wear. Sammy was thrilled.

"Thanks, Dad! And Mom!" he blubbered, as he fought back tears of joy. He gathered up all the parts, no longer interested in seeing what anybody else got. He just wanted to get it all to the basement workshop and get started on it.

"Hold it, young man!" Kenneth said, and caught him by the tail of his Superman pajamas. "Wait until your other sisters open their gifts, too. You have all of Christmas break to work on it so waiting a few more minutes won't hurt you."

Sammy's lip poked out again in the familiar pout, but he sat back down, feigning interest in the other gifts.

Abigail and Annanell got matching wall mirrors for their room. Abigail's was pink and Annanell's was blue. They were designed to look much like the magic mirror in *Snow White and the Seven Dwarfs*. The frames, with their luscious loops of whipped color, looked as though they had been made of large mounds of divinity candy. The attached shelf protruded just far enough to hold the miniature Snow White, and miniature dwarfs that came with it.

"There is something in the basement to go with the mirrors," Kenneth declared.

In excitement, the girls ran from the room to the basement. Their squeals could be heard up in the living room, and Nell and Kenneth exchanged pleased glances.

"Mom! Dad! They're beautiful! Just what we wanted!" The girls exclaimed as they rushed back into the living room. The vanity tables and chairs to match made them feel all grown up and almost as "old" as Kendra. The chairs were covered with velvet; one in pink, one in blue to match the mirrors.

Nell gathered up the wrappings and put them in the fire, now roaring in the fireplace. Sammy disappeared into the basement, the girls went up to their rooms, and Kendra and Millie curled up in front of the fire to nap.

Kenneth gathered his wife into his arms, and together they went upstairs to exchange their gifts to one another in private. This was always their time together and the rest of the family respected that. Nell would find a tiny box on the bed and Kenneth would find a box on his nightstand.

Their gifts to one another were always special things they found for one another that held special meaning in their lives. Things like restoring an old, dearly loved photograph of some event or loved one, or a piece of jewelry with a special meaning, like the solid gold apple on a chain Kenneth gave Nell recalling how they met in New York, *the Big Apple*. And there was the little bell with the diamond clapper on a chain given in remembrance of the church bells that rang the day they married.

One Christmas, it was an oil painting of their wedding picture copied from a black and white photograph. But this Christmas, it was a memory book of Kendra that Nell, with great love, had put together to give to Kenneth. A Book of Life to be completed when Kendra married and moved out of the house, *closing one chapter and opening another*, she told him.

And Kenneth gave Nell a beautiful, four-part, gold locket brooch. Pinned in place on a dress, it looked like a regular locket, but push the tiny button on the side, and four parts on hinges opened up. In each section, Kenneth had placed a picture of one of their four children, and underneath each picture was a tiny mounting of that child's birthstone.

Christmas time 1957 was a happy time indeed for the Tinker family! Their prayer at the dinner table that day was that it could always be this way.

Nine

With Christmas break over, Kendra threw herself into her studies and her work. Only one semester to go and she would be graduating. With a good job and marriage ahead for her, she was thankful that her life was progressing as she had hoped.

But for now, every bit of spare time she had, she spent in planning the wedding of her dreams. She picked out the dresses for Annanell and Abigail. They were ice blue crystalette with puffed sleeves and princess lines in the ballerina length. They went to Burt's Shoes on Main Street and had satin shoes dyed to match. She picked out their tiara headpieces to match hers, only a smaller version. She ordered pink fans with streamers of blue and pink to be gathered into a cluster of feathered pink carnations for them to carry. Everything was coming together perfectly.

Nell and Edwina went shopping and color coordinated their dresses to match; Nell wearing blue, and Edwina, pink. Kenneth spoke to the custodian of the church and asked that all the light bulbs in the church sanctuary be changed to blue bulbs.

Kendra asked Sarah to light the candles (one of the girls would help her) and her dress was a deeper blue, to match the maid of honor's dress. Kendra's maid of honor was a college friend, Eileen with whom she had gone all the way through school. They had been best friends since kindergarten. Eileen was getting married in the fall.

There was so much to do; the florist, the reception, the invitations, the rehearsal supper, finding a place to live, and the honeymoon. Tuxedo rentals had to be made well in advance and there were showers being planned almost daily for her.

"May I go to the shower the church has planned for us?" Keith asked her after the shower had been announced.

"I would love to have you sit right there by me as I open gifts!"

The shower at the church was well attended and the two received everything they needed to set up housekeeping. Keith sat beside Kendra and helped open all the gifts.

Her fellow employees hosted a kitchen shower for her, and her friends at school gave her a lingerie shower. Finding a place to store all the gifts until time to move was a problem.

"Don't worry," Nell told her, "We'll stack them on the dining room table for now." The dining room began to look like a department store!

Keith read the want ads daily trying to find a suitable apartment that would be close enough to both their places of work. Keith sent resumes to dozens of school districts,

The Passing Of Paradise   Molly Lemmons

and was waiting for interviews pending completion of his graduate work.

"Let's go early Saturday morning to look at some apartments, Kendra," Keith asked her on the phone one evening.

"All right," Kendra replied. "I'll be ready when you come by."

Early next morning, Kendra eased out of bed so as not to disturb the sleeping Millie, and quickly dressed to go "apartment hunting."

Millie opened one eye, peering at Kendra and seeing her up and out of bed, opened both eyes wide, and quickly joined her. She couldn't miss out on *anything*. It always amazed Kendra how the little thing could keep up such a pace. After all, she was getting on in years for a cat.

Keith came by precisely at 8:00 as he said he would. Kendra bounced out to his car and a quick kiss on the cheek had them on their way.

After about six tries, they were about to give up when Keith said there was one more he wanted to see. Situated on two acres, it was a house, not in the country, but with a country setting.

"A perfect place for Millie to roam free," Keith stated nonchalantly.

"But Keith, Millie is an *inside cat*; she has never been outdoors, unless I am with her. She couldn't survive outside."

Dark clouds filled Keith eyes once again and the storm began to brew inside them that Kendra had, by now, often seen but refused to address.

The Passing Of Paradise   Molly Lemmons

"Well, she will be an outside cat when we marry!" he snarled. And he shoved her, forcing her against the car door with a powerful shove.

"Keith, you can't mean that! Daddy gave Millie to me for my birthday several years ago, and she has been a constant friend and companion since that time. I couldn't just push her out and into a strange environment to be confused and lost."

"Well, she is *not* a person, and the sooner you realize that, the better for both of us. She will *not* be in the house."

Tears began to well up in Kendra's eyes again as she thought of her trusted friend.

Then again, suddenly and without warning, Keith stopped the car in front of the house and pulled her close.

"It's okay, sweetheart," he said sweetly, the black depths of his eyes returning to their soft brown again. "I didn't mean it; Millie can be wherever you want her to be. I love *you,* Kendra, so I *will love your cat, too.*"

And he held her and kissed the tears away from her eyes. The tenderness that he displayed at that moment was as *kind* as the *outburst* had been *unkind.* How a man could have two such opposite personalities all at the same time was bewildering to Kendra, but a puzzle that her love for him kept her from trying to solve. Besides, once in his arms, all memories of such incidents just dissolved.

"Let's go look inside," Keith asked, the events of the last few moments now erased as though they never happened.

They walked up the front steps and found the door unlocked.

The moment they opened the door, they both knew it was going to be "their place."

"Wait, Kendra," and Keith swooped her up and carried her across the threshold.

"Keith, you'll have to do it all over again. We aren't married yet!"

And she giggled with delight as he set her down.

"It'll be my pleasure to do it all over again," and he kissed her.

Once inside, they found it had three bedrooms, two baths, a dining room, living room, and kitchen. It also had a patio off the dining room, and the yard was large enough for a lot of flowers and also a vegetable garden. A two-car garage set back behind the house a short distance and it had extra space for a workbench. There was also enough space to store Keith's motorcycle.

Keith took the realtor's card off the kitchen cabinet and put it in his pocket.

"I'll call about it just as soon as I get back," he promised.

Ten

Kendra's workday at Kerr's involved getting there every day around 2:00 p.m. and working 'til closing time. She was so happy, she got up singing every morning. She not only loved her new job, she loved her schoolwork as well. Usually, she just went straight to work from school, not having time to go home first.

One day, during class with Sarah, while the others were working on different interests, the receptionist came and asked her to come to the desk to take a phone call. Excusing herself, Kendra went to the desk and picked up the waiting phone.

"Hello, this is Kendra," she began.

"Did you *really* think you could hide, Miss Priss?" The familiar voice began. "I know all there is to know about you—and I intend to..."

Kendra's heart sank, as she hung up the phone. She couldn't stop the flood of tears as she collapsed into the lounge chair. *I just as well give it up,* she thought. *He is not going to quit.* The receptionist knew something was very wrong but Kendra assured her it was "nothing that I can't handle," and she returned to her class.

It was hard to concentrate on her lessons, knowing that the caller was once again on her trail. She had to think about how to handle this. She didn't have Judy to help her and she didn't want Mr. Fuller to think she couldn't handle herself under pressure. In sheer numbness, she finally called it a day.

With her wedding less than six weeks away, Kendra felt she could never get everything done. And now she had to deal with this growing threat. She decided to tell Keith and see if he could help her.

Keith turned ashen when she told him of the returning caller.

"Keith, if this starts all over again, it will affect my job performance, and I can't have that. Isn't there *something* you can do?"

"Don't you worry, baby. I told you I would take care of it before and I will take care of it this time, too."

Kendra hadn't realized that Keith had "taken care of it before"—she only knew that the calls had stopped. Well, it really didn't matter to her, just so they got stopped and she could rest assured they wouldn't keep coming.

The phone calls for Kendra at work stopped, and with all she had on her mind, she soon forgot the incident. Keith called with the news that they got the house and that he had put down the first three months' rent. They could start moving in all of the gifts and could begin to look for furniture.

Kendra sent out the invitations and the list just grew bigger and bigger. Everything was taking shape now and she had to go back up to the Bridal Suite at Kerr's and try on the altered dress for one last fitting. A few details for closure and all would be set.

Betty met her as she got off the elevator and came into the parlor of the Bridal Suite.

"Let's try on your dress, Miz Scarlet," she commented, smiling. She escorted Kendra to the fitting room where the dress was hanging on a door hook. It was even more beautiful than Kendra remembered it to be.

When it floated down over the hoop, Betty buttoned all of the buttons in back. Standing back and looking from all mirrors, Kendra's small waist looked even smaller with the altered seams hugging it close to her tiny form.

"Perfect, just perfect!" Betty exclaimed with excitement. And Kendra had to agree. It was a most beautiful gown and the buoyancy of it made it appear to float as she turned this way and that, observing it from every angle. Her headpiece was also ready and she tried it on gasping at its twinkling beauty. She truly felt like a queen.

And as if reading her mind, Betty quipped, "My lands, girl, you look like a *queen!*"

Kendra paid the layaway and Betty encased the dress in a protective plastic, zippered case along with the veil, tiara, hoop, merry widow, and crinoline. Kendra carried her precious cargo to her car and headed home. Nell would be picking up the attendants' dresses when their alterations were complete.

Kendra sang on the way home, "I give you my love, My Love, for as long as I live..." And she kept singing it over and over all the way home. This would be a surprise for Keith, for he didn't know that she had written a song to sing to him at the wedding.

Spring came and everything began to bud out. The days were getting longer and warmer and graduation day was upon Kendra. She just hoped that she could get everything done in time with so much happening. Her graduation day was just two weeks before her wedding and trying to juggle two such grand occasions had Kendra exhausted just thinking about it.

Nell, Kenneth, and the children were proud as they sat at Kendra's graduation. They listened for what seemed a long time to faculty members describe the honors and awards their daughter had achieved, before she walked across the stage to accept her diploma. Keith sat beside them, also beaming with pride. He took her to a special supper afterwards where the two could be together alone.

It was a beautiful night to remember. He gave her a charm for her bracelet, a small piano with keys that actually moved up and down. The enclosed card read: *"You will always be the music in my soul, my dearest Kendra, and I will love you as long as I live. You have made my life worth living. Keith."*

Kendra opened it as they sat at the restaurant, and people watching or not, she couldn't contain herself. On impulse, she threw her arms around Keith's neck and hugged him tight—really tight. So tight that she embarrassed herself and quickly pulled away.

"It's okay, I don't care who sees us. I love you!" and he pulled her back into his arms. "Just two weeks from tonight, my precious, and you will be *mine*!"

Kendra felt loved and safe as Keith held her, right there in public, and she didn't care a bit.

Eleven

On the morning of May twenty-fourth, Kendra was up early and going about tending to last minute details of her wedding. The rehearsal supper was scheduled to be at *Beverly's Hideaway Restaurant* located in a private, secluded area of North Oklahoma City, and there were a few last minute details to consider. Counting everyone in the wedding party, Cal and Edwina would be hosting about twenty-five guests at the supper.

One last check on the menu, and Kendra was glad to see that Keith's father had ordered prime rib, baked potatoes, salad, rolls, and a vegetable medley, topped off with cheesecake for dessert. It made her smile to see that Cal was being cooperative after all.

She arrived at the church early to see if the flowers were being put into place, check on the music, and be sure everything was being decorated for the reception that would be held in the church's overflow room.

A bit nervous and excited, she was overwhelmed with the beauty of the inside of the church as she walked into the auditorium. Caesar's Flower Shop was working on decorating the stage with pink gladiolas and lots of greenery. Silver candelabras with blue candles stood stately in the background, waiting to be lit. All of the ordinarily white light bulbs in the ceiling and along the outside walls of the auditorium had been replaced with blue ones. Kendra couldn't wait for dark to see how they would look.

Nell picked up the dress after having it steamed and Kenneth picked up the tuxedoes. They put them in the dressing room at the church. Everything was falling into place for the moment of Kendra's dreams.

That night at the rehearsal, Kendra and Keith just went numbly through the motions. Both were so caught up in the excitement and beauty of it all, that by the time the wedding party arrived at the restaurant, they barely remembered what had taken place. Kendra did not tell him about the song she had written for him. That was to be her wedding gift to him and he would not know about it until she began to sing it.

"That's so stupid," Sammy grumbled, "To sing a dumb old song! How embarrassing!" And he moaned and groaned and put his hands over his ears.

"Someday you will understand, little brother," Kendra reminded him, and she scrubbed his noggin.

"Aw, stop it, Sis. You messed up my hair."

After the rehearsal supper, a tired bride-to-be fell into bed. Millie sensed the fatigue of her mistress and snuggled closer than ever to her and purred loudly as if to comfort her.

Early the next morning, Keith called.

"Hi, baby, let's go over to the house and finish unpacking. I'll pick you up in a few minutes."

"Give me about an hour; I just woke up. I have a beauty shop appointment in a little while, so I can't be gone too long."

"Okay—I'll be by about 8:00—love you, bye!"

Kendra slowly rolled out of bed and dressed. She thought it was bad luck to see the groom the day of the wedding, but they really did still have a lot to do, so she agreed to go help Keith with the unpacking. She really thought those things could wait until they returned from their honeymoon, but if that was what he wanted to do now, she would do it.

At 8:00, Keith rang the bell.

"Mom! Keith is here. We're going over to the house and take the rest of the gifts. I'll be back in time to go to the beauty shop with you!" Kendra called.

As she opened the door, Millie wasn't far behind, and as always lodged herself between the curtains and the window glass to watch Kendra and Keith leave.

She didn't budge until the car was out of sight. Then with sadness, she jumped down and laid by the door to wait for Kendra's return. She stayed closer than ever to Kendra, seeming to *sense* what was to come.

The house was taking shape, and beginning to look like "home" to Keith and Kendra. Nell had made curtains for the windows—all sixteen of them—and she and Kenneth had already hung them. The carpet had been shampooed, and the furniture was in place. Kenneth managed to get enough help to even move the baby grand piano over to the house, giving the house the crowning finishing touch that Kendra needed. Many hours of practice were spent at that piano, and to keep her talent polished, Kendra never neglected that need.

Groceries were in the cabinets, and the refrigerator was full of goodies. It had been a family effort; all of them working together, making it ready for occupancy once the couple returned from their honeymoon. Nell had baked bread, pies, and cookies for storage in the pantry, and the little girls, who were learning to embroider, had made some cup towels. Even Sammy had helped by cleaning the oil spots from the garage floor and Kenneth had mowed the lawn and had the flowerbeds and garden spots tilled and ready for planting.

As Keith and Kendra unpacked the final load, they realized it was getting late.

"I've got to get to the beauty shop, Keith!"

"I have just one request—*please do not wear your hair up.* I want to see it rippling around your shoulders under your veil when you come down the isle. Okay?"

"Well, I'm glad you told me. I *was* going to wear it up in a cluster of ringlets, but if you want it down, then down it will be." And she stood on her tiptoes and kissed him on the cheek. Keith beamed his approval.

Kendra drove to the beauty shop where her mother was waiting for her with just minutes to spare before her appointment.

"Mom, I've decided to wear my hair down, so all I need is a shampoo and time under the dryer."

"When did you decide *that?* I thought you were going to wear it up and the tiara around the cluster."

"Keith wants it down and I can wear the tiara like a crown, just on top of my head," Kendra answered.

The two women were finished by 4:00. They had four hours to be sure all was in order and to get dressed. Together they went to the church building to mark their checklist. Everything looked beautiful! The reception area was decorated in blue ribbons with pink carnations on every table. The glowing pink and blue candles cast romantic shadows across the room. The caterer had them all lit, checking to see if the look was "just right." "We'll leave the lights out during the reception," she said. "By the time we come in here, it will be dark enough outside that having the candle light only, will make the mood just as you want it, Kendra."

The cake was elegant. Enough to serve over five hundred people, the wedding was planned to accommodate the large crowd, as the invitation list had just kept growing and growing.

Kendra was too excited to sit down. She flitted from room to room, chattering about everything and nothing.

"Kendra, settle down. You're as nervous as Millie gets when she sees the neighbors' dogs cross the yard!"

"Oh, Mom, I just want it all to be so *perfect!*"

"It will be, sweetheart; now calm down."

Kendra didn't know where they were going for their honeymoon. Keith had simply said, "It's a surprise, but pack clothes for warmth."

She had her luggage packed and Keith was going to pick it up while she was at the church. He hid his car in a safe place and his best man would be sure that the luggage got packed in it.

"Mom, I think I better start getting ready. It's late."

Nell and Kendra went into the church dressing area where there were full-length mirrors on every wall.

Suddenly, Kendra threw her arms around her mother.

"Oh, Mom, this is the day I have dreamed all of my life!" She sighed as she giggled, and blushed in embarrassment as she thought of what she was about to say.

"You know, when I first learned about 'life,' I used to worry that I might die before I got to see what *'it'* is like." Kendra just kept on hugging her mother as tight as she could. She didn't want Nell to see her blush, but Nell felt the heat from her daughter's cheek against her face.

Nell was well aware of what her daughter was talking about. She had drilled into Kendra the morals that her mother before *her* had drilled into *her*, and she knew exactly how Kendra felt. In fact, she could recall telling her own mother the very same thing on her wedding day.

"Oh, my dear Kendra, you are such a treasure to your father and me. You have never disappointed us, and our prayer for you is that you receive all the good things back that you have so unselfishly given. Whatever lies ahead for you, just remember that we love you and will be here for you should you ever need us. Now, let's get that little body of yours dressed in this gown and get you ready to receive the love of your life."

"Mom, I love you and Daddy so much. Thank you for everything you've taught me. I understand so much more now—all the reasons for what you've taught me. I may have seemed ungrateful and rebellious at times, but it was all just a part of growing up and becoming my own person. I'm thankful that you never gave in to me. I now know that what you both have given me is a part of yourselves, and I'll always love you for it."

Nell turned away and brushed the tears back as she took Kendra's dress off the hanger. Kendra slipped into the merry widow and Nell hooked it. Instantly, another inch was nipped off Kendra's already tiny waist.

Kendra stretched out each of the four tiers of the bamboo slats that widened the hoop to capacity, and slipped the swinging hoop skirt on over her head.

"Hold up your arms, dear," Nell told her, and she lowered the starched organdy crinoline in place on top of the hoop.

Next came the dress. The beautiful dress. Nell helped to smooth out all the folds in its skirt so that the entire width of it could be fully appreciated as it lay over the hoop.

"I'm in a hurry, Mom. Just button every other button."

"Kendra! This is *not* dress rehearsal. This is the *real thing*. I will *not* button *'every other button.'*" And she stifled a giggle.

Kendra was jittery as Nell patiently buttoned all eighty-five buttons down the back and helped her button the ten buttons running up each sleeve cuff.

Kendra wanted to wear the veil over her face as tradition called for the blush of the bride to be covered until the minister pronounced them married.

Nell situated the tiara on top of her daughter's head, and secured the combs tightly into her hair. Then with a tremendous amount of love and care, she eased the upper layer of tulle over Kendra's face, but it couldn't hide the beauty of her golden/red hair, or the sweet expression of happiness on her face.

Kendra had chosen this room in which to dress because she wanted just her mother with her. The rest of the wedding party was dressing in another room further down the hall.

The caterer knocked on the door.

"We're lining up the wedding party now."

The building was full. The blue lights glowed softly and the atmosphere was one of *reverenc*e as Kendra got in line. It was quiet except for the sweet strains of the beginning song, *My God and I,* Kendra's favorite.

When the wedding march began, Kendra started down the isle on her father's arm. She saw Keith waiting at the end of the long walk and he almost lost his breath when he saw her. Never had he thought her to be more beautiful than at this moment. He felt he was the luckiest man alive—a woman to love who was as pure as she was beautiful.

"Who gives this woman to be married to this man?"

"Her mother, her sisters, her brother, and *I do*," was Kenneth's answer.

Kenneth took his seat beside Nell, and Kendra moved next to Keith.

Their vows were the age-old vows repeated many times every year in the little church of Christ where Kendra had grown up. There were people in the audience that had known her since her birth, and she felt as though they were family.

She promised to love Keith in sickness, health, for better or worse, in good times and bad, and he in turn, promised her to do the same. Just before the minister pronounced them married, Kendra turned to Keith and began to sing her wedding song that she had written just for him. The melody floated across the auditorium and mesmerized the audience with its simple beauty. No one could sing like Kendra Tinker. Keith never once took his eyes off her. It was clear that he loved her as much as she loved him.

"I now pronounce you man and wife. You may kiss your bride, Keith."

Keith turned to Kendra and eased the veil off her face, draping it behind her. Then he took her into his arms and very carefully, slowly and tenderly kissed her. She held to him, as much because she loved him, as she did because of the weakness in her knees. She was afraid she might fall down the stairs as she stepped off the stage.

Almost five hundred people went through the receiving line to congratulate the young couple. It was nearly midnight by the time they shook the last hand, and hugged the last neck. Kendra told her parents and siblings goodbye, and went to change her clothes. They had a plane to catch.

Annanell and Abigail fought the tears, and Sammy just shrugged. "It was way too mushy," he grumbled.

Kendra chose her pink lace dress with the full skirt and high lace collar and puffed sleeves for travel. She was wearing the pink corsage that was pinned in the center of her bouquet before she tossed it.

The car was waiting and the crowd showered them with rice as they climbed in and sped away.

"Where're we going?" Kendra asked.

"You'll see," and Keith just kept on driving and grinning.

He pulled her close and kissed her. Once or twice the car swerved sideways.

"Keith, people will think we're drunk!"

"Nope, not with that *just married* sign scrawled out in big letters on the back," he laughed. They parked the car for Nell and Kenneth to pick up later and barely made the run to the plane as it was loading out on the runway.

Twelve

The honeymoon package that Keith put together for Kendra was the one with a darling Victorian-style cottage snuggled in total seclusion in the mountains of Colorado. The taxi service that Keith had reserved was waiting to take them to their cottage when they got off the plane. When the driver let them out and they unloaded their luggage, both bounced out and ran up the stairs to the deck. The top floor housed the bedroom, bath, and sunroom, and the glass shower stall was free standing out under the stars at the corner of the deck. Management had everything ready for them—low music was playing, and the soft glow of the hurricane lamps with their pink rose taffeta shades with the ecru lace edges, cast soft, flickering shadows over the room. The fire in the fireplace was crackling its warm welcome as well as the one in the downstairs living area.

Just as Kendra started to open the sliding glass patio doors, Keith stopped her.

"Ah, ah, ah, my little precious, stop where you are!"

And he swooped her up into his arms to carry her over the threshold and into the bedroom. He kissed her passionately, then very gently set her down.

"Now you are officially mine, Mrs. Kouch," he said proudly. Kendra gasped at the beauty she saw there. The magnificent heart shaped bed was covered with a pink-rose taffeta spread and the pillow shams were edged in ecru lace. The drapes were rose sheers with pink-rose taffeta linings, and a valance of solid ecru lace. The carpet was a plush, dusty rose, with a thick, cushioned pad that sank down when they walked. The bedroom walls were covered with mirrors that reflected the beauty from a two hundred-crystal prisms chandelier that hung from the center of the ceiling over the bed.

"Oh, Keith, it's perfectly charming! It's like a dream come true for me. Oh, thank you, thank you, so very much."

Keith brought in the luggage and set it down in the middle of the bedroom floor.

"For the next five days, Kendra, we will concentrate only on each other. I have so many plans for the two of us."

Kendra began to unpack the luggage and to hang the clothes in the closet. It was just a few hours until sunrise by now, but neither of them felt sleepy or tired. Keith went over to stoke the fire and turn back the bed. Kendra picked up her overnight bag and disappeared into the bathroom.

Once inside and with the door closed, she began to tremble. She took off her going-away dress and hung it up carefully. Slowly, she unfolded the beautiful negligee her mother had given her for her wedding night. The gown was white with ribbon straps, embossed with pink satin roses and hearts and the skirt was the sheerest nylon with tiny little pleats in the swirling skirt. The robe dipped to a "v" in the back from which hung a pink satin ribbon with long streamers, and the neckline was edged with roses and hearts.

Keith knocked at the door. "Kendra, what's taking you so long?"

Surely she *was* taking awhile, and on purpose. She was nervous and her heart pounded so hard in her chest, she wondered if Keith could hear it. Excited at the prospect of all she had waited and dreamed about, when the precise moment came, she was suddenly very timid. Her mind raced with questions, and fears. *What if I am a disappointment to him? What if he regrets choosing me? What if he doesn't think me attractive? What if I don't know what to do? Will he be patient? Will he be angry?* The doubts were scaring her. She wondered if Eve had been afraid.

"It'll be just a minute more."

"Honey, please come out." And pressing his face close to the door, he whispered, "Don't take off your dress. I want that privilege."

Kendra shivered. She could barely think. She had already removed her traveling dress.

"Keith, will you turn out the lights?"

"Anything for you..."

With the lights off, only the warm glow of the burning fire illuminated the room. Quickly, Kendra brushed through her hair and slowly opened the door. Like a shy little girl, she peeked from behind it, and felt her face blush as pink as the roses on her gown.

"Sweetheart, you're beautiful!" and taking her in his arms, he picked her up and carried her to the bed, placing her with care on the pink satin sheets. Lying beside her, he pulled her close and kissed her. With Keith holding her, all of Kendra's questions and fears vaporized with the gentle kindness of his touch. Her mind spun with swirls of midnight blue, plunging her into a semi-conscious world of sublime happiness, and she knew that Keith would always be the center of that world!

~ * ~

Sunlight streaming into their bedroom windows, covering them with its golden glory awoke them a few hours later. It was going to be a beautiful day to begin their new life.

The entire week was filled with many good things. There were walks in the snow, dining at romantic restaurants, and sitting together on the deck. In the evening, they watched the deer with their fawns come out to graze the tiny seedlings poking their heads through the melting snow. They talked of many things; the family they wanted to have some day, the home they planned to build, and the dreams they would have for their children. There was never a hint of the mood changes Kendra had seen in Keith as they dated, leading her to believe she had imagined a big part of it, or maybe even overacted to what she thought happened. Her love for Keith was so deep, so real, that it could mask even a hint of anything that could be wrong.

All too soon, the week was over, and it was time to go home.

The taxi waited outside while Kendra and Keith took one last "scope" of the little cottage that had been their home for one week. They walked through the living area and checked out the kitchen for anything left in the refrigerator, then made a quick run up the stairs. They stood, holding hands, as they glanced over the room, both of them putting an indelible memory of every detail of the last week into their minds. With a tinge of sadness, they picked up the luggage as the driver began to honk, losing his patience.

It had been the happiest time of Kendra's life. She had a lot of blessings and good memories of family and friends, but being with Keith for that first wonderful week, summarized all of everything good she had ever felt. How thankful to God she was for her blessings!

Thirteen

"Mom! We're home!" Kendra couldn't wait to tell her parents what a wonderful time they had in Colorado. Even before she helped Keith unload the car, she ran into the house to call.

"Oh, Mom, everything was just so perfect—and Colorado is such a gorgeous state! I wish you and Daddy could go sometime—you'd love it!"

"Okay, Kendra, help me unload the car, then you can talk," Keith called from the utility room as he came in dragging suitcases.

"Gotta go, Mom. Tell Daddy and the kids hello and that we are back safe and sound. We'll come by tomorrow and pick up Millie. Talk to you later. Love you. Bye."

Kendra thought of the hundreds of thank you notes she needed to write and all the unpacking she had to do and she got tired just thinking about it. Mr. Fuller had graciously given her three extra days to get caught up before she had to go back to work and Keith had also taken off extra days from his job as Superintendent of the Bel Isle Public Schools in nearby Moore, Oklahoma. He got the job just before the wedding and was thrilled that the school board hired him, allowed him to take days off so soon, and also for permitting him to finish his Ph.D. at his convenience.

"Okay, baby, get a move on, and let's get this mess put away! I want to go for a spin on my motorcycle before it gets too late!"

Kendra opened the suitcases and began to put in laundry and to hang up clothes. Keith put on his helmet and went out to the garage to get his Harley. She heard him rev up the motor and heard the crunch of the gravel as he sped out the drive. She listened until she couldn't hear the sound of the bike anymore.

It grew dark and Keith was not home. Kendra began to get worried. She ran a tub full of hot water and poured in bubble bath until the bubbles were peaking to a frothy cap of six inches. She pinned up her hair and slowly eased herself into the hot suds. She lay back on her foam pillow and closed her eyes. She tried to relax, but the thoughts swirling inside her head made it almost impossible because she was a little more than just worried. She reached over the edge of the tub and turned on WKY Radio. *Your Hit Parade* had just come on. Just as Jo Stafford began to sing "*You Belong to Me*," she heard the putter-putter of the cycle as it came to an abrupt stop just outside the garage door. She got out of the tub in a hurry, wrapped the plush sheet towel around her and rushed out to greet Keith, barefoot and still soaking wet. Throwing her arms around him, she hugged him with all her might, almost losing the towel in the process.

"Oh, Keith, I was so worried about you! Where were you so long? Oh, sweetie, you've bruised your jaw. Did you have a wreck?" She moved to kiss his jaw.

For just an instant, the eyes darkened, but quickly lightened back up and Keith forced a grin.

"I took a little tumble and I really don't have to give an account to you of where I was, Miss Kendra, but for your information, I went to see an old friend. I had a debt to pay. I owed it before we left and told him I would pay him when I returned."

"Do I know him?"

"What difference does it make?"

"What did you owe him?"

"Just an old debt from a while back that I had almost forgotten about. Don't you worry your pretty little head about it... let's go get you in some dry clothes, your teeth are chattering.

He rolled the cycle into the garage and put down the kickstand. He closed the garage door, lifted Kendra into his arms and cuddling her close, carried her to the house.

When they neared the kitchen door, Keith said, "Let's go raid the pantry—but first, let me take off that towel and unclip your hair."

While still in his arms, Keith slowly unwound the towel and gently removed the clip from Kendra's hair. Her hair tumbled down in cascades below her shoulders, and the damp ringlets framed her face in hundreds of curly-cues. Keith put her down gently, allowing the towel to drop to the floor. In the moments to follow, Kendra didn't recall worrying about anything after all.

But later, when they went into the kitchen, Kendra put a loving hand on Keith's cheek.

"Sweetheart, you need to tend that bruise."

"Well, *sweetheart*," he said mocking her, "You need to tend your own business!" and his eyes sank into the pit of darkness. This time, they didn't recede immediately. Instead, the old familiar look appeared and Kendra was afraid.

Tears filled her eyes and she turned and walked away. Keith grabbed her hair and pulled her to him. He jerked her head backwards and glaring directly into her face began to scream.

"If I want you to know something, I will tell you—you will *not* be a nosey wife. If I choose not to tell you something, it will be none of your business. Do you understand? *No woman* will be my boss—not even *you!*"

Kendra didn't know what to do. This was real, wasn't it? *Wasn't it?* All she could do was sob. Just a few minutes before this, he had made love to her and told her over and over how very much he loved her.

Then suddenly, Keith took her into his arms, smoothed her hair and gently kissed her as the surge of anger subsided. Then as though nothing had happened, he quietly told her, "Let's see what your mom left in the pantry for us to eat." And he brought out all the goodies to snack on that Kenneth and Nell had put there when the newlyweds had left on their honeymoon.

"Umm, this looks good. Come on, baby, join me."

Kendra was again puzzled. Had she imagined it? Was she going crazy?

"Put on the white gown with the pink roses and hearts—you're a princess in that, Kendra. I love to just look at you. You're the best thing to ever happen to me. Don't you ever forget that." Again, Kendra's thoughts were interrupted.

The next morning, Kendra popped out of bed to make her man a very special breakfast. It was hard to slip out of his strong arms but she was able to do it without waking him. But first, she wanted to practice the piano. She wanted to wake him up with the song she wrote for their wedding. She sang through it once, then again. Keith stayed still, pretending to still be sleeping, just so she would keep singing it. He loved it when she started their day with a song, and she did that most every morning.

"Keith! Breakfast is ready!" she called from the kitchen.

A stretching, yawning Keith slipped behind her and engulfed her with a mammoth hug and picked her up and swung her around.

"Keith, put me down and let's eat breakfast. We need to go over to the folks' house and pick up Millie. I know she's lonesome to see me and we need to get her used to her new home. She's never been out of our house so this will be an adjustment."

"Okay, Kendra. I'll bet she's had that little pink nose pressed against the living room window ever since we left! Her motor will run overtime when she sees you after so long! It'll be cute watching her." And he laughed a genuine, caring, laugh.

Sure enough, when Keith and Kendra drove up to Nell and Kenneth's house, the curtains moved, and there next to the window was the little white Persian with the sky blue eyes, her nose pressed against the glass!

"She's been there almost the entire time you were gone," Nell said as she greeted her daughter and new son-in-law. Of course when she saw Kendra, Millie raced off the windowsill and bounced around like a jumping bean until Kendra picked her up.

"Oh, Millie, if you could talk, you would be saying 'I love you, Kendra,'" and truly she *was* saying it in the only way she knew how: with purrs and chirps and throaty 'owwwsss.'

"You're going to a new home, Millie, so just get ready for it." And she scratched Millie's throat as the cat peered directly into her face.

Kenneth came in from his study and greeted the couple, hugging his daughter and shaking his son-in-law's hand.

Kendra's chatting had no end as she talked about the wonderful week they had just shared, and one by one, the three children came to listen. Annabelle and Abigail came and quietly sat on the floor, hands clasped around their doubled-up knees and listened, mesmerized. The stories of the gentle deer and their babies, of the gorgeous mountains and streams, the snowball fights and making angels in the snow captivated them.

The pictures of all of the wild life, the description of the night sky with its uninterrupted total blackness, peppered with a "zillion" diamond-like stars, and the incredible sunrises and sunsets, kept even Sammy's attention. Even though he slouched down in the recliner and pretended not to listen, the truth be known, he loved every bit of it.

"Can you imagine a night sky where there are no town lights to reflect on the clouds to dim how many stars there are up there?" Kendra asked.

"If you were of a mind to, you could count stars until the end of time and never get them all counted. We could see every star there was to see! Made us feel small and insignificant in such a vast scope of creation. The sky was *black* and the stars stood out so crisp and clear. God feels very near in the mountains."

"We better load up and head home, honey. Scoop up that little cat and let's get going."

Kendra gathered up Millie, her toys, food and dishes and her pillow, told her parents goodnight, and headed to the car.

"Well, it's back to work Monday, Kendra. Have you had a good time?"

"Oh, Keith, you *know* I have!"

They turned into their drive. Kendra handed Millie to Keith and got out to open the garage door. The squirming cat finally settled herself in Keith's lap and he drove the car inside.

Kendra unloaded the car and the three headed up to the house.

"Well, this little stinker is going to have quite an adjustment now, isn't she, Kendra?"

"Yes, but she is very intelligent. Won't take her long to catch on."

Kendra was right. Millie settled herself right square in the middle of the bed and purred herself to sleep the very first night away from the only house she had ever known.

Monday morning Kendra kissed Keith goodbye and he left to go to work. She finished up the breakfast dishes, fed Millie, and prepared to leave in her car. She was a little anxious to get back to her work. Sarah, her favorite student would be ready and waiting for her when she got there. Sarah had been in an abusive environment, where her tremendous musical talent had been squelched. An older couple, unable to have any more children after the loss of a little girl, had adopted her and vowed to see to it that her talent was developed to the fullest. Because Kendra recognized that ability also, the little girl was responsive and eager to learn. When she sat at the piano, Kendra had to fight tears because Sarah was almost totally blind from the abuse, and yet she could make the "ivory talk." Her dream was to play at Carnegie Hall, and Kendra had no doubt she would make it. As she played, her face glowed with happiness from within, and she appeared to be of another time and another place.

It was because Kendra loved Sarah so much that she wanted to help her be all that she could be. The innocence of this child and the beauty of her soul reached out to Kendra and brought out the best in her.

~ * ~

"Now Millie, you behave and I'll see you this afternoon."

Kendra closed the door and the kitten took up her vigil at her new station in front of the kitchen window, her eyes following Kendra until she was out of sight.

Sure enough, as Kendra expected, Sarah was at the registration desk when she arrived. She was almost forty-five minutes early just as Kendra knew she would be. The other students would be arriving just as the whistle blew with barely time to get out their instruments. But not Sarah. Music was her life and she had the determination and ability to see that it remained that way. That's why she had chosen a twelve-month school year, with only a small break between sessions. It was through her music that she *lived... really lived.*

Keith returned to his office to find it full of all colors of balloons and cards and well wishes. His staff gathered around to welcome him back, and he felt much appreciated.

In the days to follow, life went on as usual; Kendra loving Keith more every day and he in turn, loving her. Every week, he honored her with flowers, jewelry, or some kind of gift commemorating their "another week anniversary."

"Oh, Keith, you're spoiling me."

"And don't you forget it. And I repeat: don't you forget that you are the best thing to ever happen to me."

Kendra glowed.

Soon summer passed into fall, and the flowers and the garden the two had put in began to die for another season.

One afternoon just as her class was about to end, the receptionist called Kendra to the phone.

Kendra immediately recognized the caller as the heavy breathing began.

"Kendra, just because you're married now, don't think I've forgotten you..." the voice began. Kendra quickly hung up the phone and burst into tears. She regained her composure and went to talk to Mr. Fuller.

"I don't know what to do, Mr. Fuller. Is there someway that you can get Roy Brown to help me when he makes the Kerr rounds?"

Mr. Fuller looked up from behind his desk, pushed his ever-sliding glasses up on his nose and the kindness in his face showed his genuine concern for Kendra.

"I'll get right on it, Kendra. Don't you worry about a thing."

That night, Kendra told Keith about the call.

This time his rage was not directed toward Kendra. It was directed toward the caller. Without a word, he grabbed his helmet, stomped out and ran to the garage.

"Keith! Where are you going?" Kendra called, but no answer. The only sound she heard was the sound of his motorcycle as he spun out the drive and into the darkness.

Kendra was confused. She walked the floor waiting for his return as the minutes ticked away. Frustrated, she picked up Millie and curled up on the divan and shook as she cuddled the kitten close.

At last, she heard the muffled sound of the cycle and saw the lights as they hit the living room curtains when he turned into the drive. She held her breath as she heard him come through the kitchen door.

"Keith! Tell me what's happening!"

"I'll tell you when you need to know," he snapped. Then silence. He closed the back door and came on in through the utility room.

With a calm air, he hung up his helmet, stuffed his gloves in his jacket pocket, slung his jacket over the washing machine lid, and sauntered nonchalantly into the kitchen. He grabbed a Coke from the refrigerator as he walked by. He pushed the bottle under the cupped edge of the opener attached to the side of the cabinet, put it to his lips, took a sip, then joined her on the divan. He snatched Millie from Kendra's lap and tossed her to the floor.

"Come here, baby, and give your husband a kiss."

Then he held her close kissing her, and all the while he whispered how much he loved her.

"That caller will never bother you again. I promise you that."

Kendra was stunned and hurt. Her questions went unanswered and each time she tried to ask, she was stopped when he pressed his mouth over hers in a passionate kiss. And as always, she was again lost in the softness of the moment and all uncertainties drifted from her memory.

The next day at work Mr. Fuller called Kendra into his office. When Kendra went inside, Roy Brown stood up from where he was sitting across from Mr. Fuller. His arm was in a sling and he had a black eye.

"Roy! What happened?" Kendra asked.

"I was painting the trim on our house and fell off the ladder. Nobody ever told me I was too old to be painting a house, but I'm all right. Jerry here tells me that the caller called you again."

"Yes, that's right, and I need your help."

"I have a pretty good lead on it, Kendra. Another one of the girls over at Brown's is getting the same thing. I think this guy migrates from store to store. We are close to wrapping it up. Just be patient with us. The young man over there who does the window displays is our prime suspect. From now on, I advise you not to answer any calls. We are hoping this will discourage him and at least keep him in one store. Try not to worry."

Kendra felt better after talking to Roy Brown. He was a good house detective and knew his business well. She was thankful for him and felt that finally, help was on the way.

Fourteen

The trees began to lose their leaves of many colors and the strong winds of Oklahoma blew them around in giant piles against the chain link fence surrounding Kendra's and Keith's home. Winter wasn't far behind and the weathermen predicted that the coming cold spell would be one unprecedented in Oklahoma's history. And they were exactly right.

When it blew in, it blew in with great force. The wind howled around the house and the snow began to fall, the wind blowing it into great drifts around the house and garage. Keith built a fire in the fireplace every night, and when they were without power for a few hours one night, they managed to stay warm and snug by the fire. The big, soft, white fleece rug in front of the fire was a cozy place to read or cuddle. It became a favorite place of Millie's, too, and she often edged her way between Kendra and Keith as they lay there side by side. The night that the temperature dropped to minus nine—a rarity for Oklahoma winters—she pushed her nose between them, and settled herself calmly in the middle and began to purr.

Kendra got the brush and began to brush her. Great wads of the soft, silky Persian fur came off in her brush.

"Millie, now you be still and let me brush out all that loose hair." The kitten lay still as a mouse, not once budging, while Kendra brushed her beautiful, coat smooth. This was a job Kendra was faithful to do so as not to agitate Keith about any loose hair. It seemed to greatly distress him, so she was very careful to always keep Millie meticulously groomed.

Suddenly, and with no warning, Keith grabbed Millie by the nape of the neck.

"This cat's going outside! I am sick to death of her always being around here, always following you around and always underfoot. She sheds and I'm sick of white cat hairs always on my clothes and furniture!" And he started toward the back door, Millie's feet dangling as she kicked and squirmed.

"No!" Kendra jumped up and ran after him. "You can't do that, Keith, she'll freeze. She's a house cat and has never experienced this kind of weather. You'll kill her!" And she ran and grabbed Keith's shirttail and pulled him back.

"Please, Keith... I love her. You know I do. Please don't do this to her!"

"Get your hands off me!" And he whirled around and slapped Kendra so hard that she fell against the corner of the kitchen cabinet and collapsed onto the floor. She tried to catch herself on the way down and twisted her wrists as she fell. She heard them crack but she felt no pain. All she could think of was saving her kitten.

The pit of darkness that arose in Keith's eyes was worse than she had ever seen. She was seeing a *maniac*, a *stranger, and she was, for the first time, admitting there was something wrong here, very wrong.*

She got up and followed Keith out to the utility room. By now, he had a tight hold on Millie's neck with his huge hand all the way around it, and was opening the back door.

Kendra ran sobbing to him and pleading, "Please Keith, I beg you. Don't hurt my little Millie. You say you love me, then why don't you love my pet?" And she pulled at his trousers, pleading over and over. He shoved her away, and she went right back and began to pound him with her fists, disregarding the swelling in her hands and wrists. She tried to take Millie out of his hands, but he held the kitten above her head with one hand, and shoved her with the other one. Millie's questioning eyes and cries of pain seemed to make Keith even angrier and he tightened his grip on Millie's throat.

His face took on an aura of evil and Kendra didn't know this man she had married. She grabbed for his hair, anything to try and stop him.

"Please, Keith, please, please."

She was frantic. Keith turned and kicked her away and stepped out into the blizzard. Holding his hand tightly around Millie's neck, he twirled her around his head like a cowboy twirls a rope, flinging her high into the air. Her neck broke in mid air, and the sound of the snap caused Kendra to collapse on the floor, limp and hysterical. Millie landed with a soft thud into the snow almost as far away as the garage. Still in a rage, Keith stomped back into the living room. Then, just as suddenly as it had appeared, his anger began to subside, and he sat down beside the fire as though nothing at all had happened.

"Come back in here beside me, my little wife," he called to Kendra. And he patted the rug and grinned the grin that had always melted her heart.

This time, it didn't work. It was time to admit that something was bad wrong with Keith Kouch. This was the last straw. She now must face reality and truth. Kendra was crying so hard that she couldn't catch her breath. As though in a trance, she snatched her coat, mittens, boots and wool cap and put them on. She was blinded with tears and sorrow as she went out the back door, grabbing her long muffler as she went out. Her hands inside the mittens were beginning to throb.

Millie was lying in the snow, her broken body limp as a rag doll. Kendra picked her up and the cold temperatures had already begun to freeze the warm little body. Cupping her hands under Millie's dangling neck, she hugged the little face to hers, rubbing the soft pink nose against her own.

"Oh, Millie, I'm so sorry, so very sorry..." she repeated, sobbing. And she wrapped the little thing in her wool muffler and placed her carefully in the flowerbed where the tulips would be coming up in the spring. She would bury her later when the ground had thawed enough to dig. She just couldn't think about that right now.

Then all of a sudden, she jumped up and ran with all her might to the garage. She opened the garage door and got in her car. She started the motor, peeled out the drive, slipping and sliding on the ice until she was out on the road. She didn't even know what direction she was going and she didn't care. She turned on the wipers but the snow was coming down so hard that it couldn't keep the windshield clean enough to see ahead. She was numb with all that had happened and the tears kept flooding and blinding her even more. All she could think of was, *Why me, Lord? Do I deserve this?* Then guilt overwhelmed her for having such a thought after all the blessings she'd been given. She bounced back and forth with questions and no answers came. Then she thought of Job and all of his trials and how he kept on keeping on. But it didn't make it any easier. She was so sad and angry at the same time; it wasn't wise for her to make any judgments at this point. She would have to wait until she could clear her head to think.

Somewhere in the back of her mind, she heard Keith calling out to her as she spun out the drive. But he was the last person in the world she wanted to see now. She didn't even want to know what he was saying to her. Probably trying to tell her how much he loved her. Well, she wouldn't fall for that ever again. She was through. But was she? Could she be? She pledged before God to love him "in sickness and health and better or worse" and Keith *was* sick!

"*No!*" she said out loud. "He is *not* sick; he is mean— being kind was an *act*! So what do I do, Lord?"

Suddenly, Kendra hit something. She didn't know what she hit because she couldn't see.

But it sent the 1954 Chevrolet Bel Air spinning off the shoulder and into a ditch. If the ditch hadn't been so full of soft, fluffy snow, she could've been badly hurt, but the snow broke the rolls of the car and it landed back upright in the ditch. Brought back out of her trance, she sat a moment in the car and tried to think what to do. There must be a farmhouse close by where she could go. She could freeze if she stayed in the car, or she could freeze trying to find help.

She buttoned up her coat, pulled the stocking cap further down and adjusted her mittens on her swollen hands. She kept the motor running, and turned the heater up as high as it would go, deciding to stay in the warm car for as long as the gasoline lasted. There wasn't much in the tank to start with so she tucked her aching hands in her coat pocket and drew up her legs to wait. The clicking of the stuck turn signal seemed to say, *Ken-dra, Ken-dra, Ken-dra*. She had never felt more alone and never so sad. The headlights cast a dim, hazy light across the snow. Maybe someone would see them before the battery ran down if the snow didn't completely cover the car, she thought. Then, all at once, the engine ground to an abrupt stop, and try as she could, it wouldn't start again. The impact had damaged the motor and no amount of trying could restart it. Her only other option was to find a farmhouse. She opened the door and the snow fell in from off the car and off the drift. She managed to plow through it and get onto what she thought was the road. She began to walk. With every step, tears began again as she thought of Millie's sweet little face and the terrible way she had died. It was so cold, her tears began to freeze. What was she going to do? The way she felt right at the moment, somehow she didn't really care. Her grief was overwhelming as she trudged along in the snow.

~ * ~

"Nell, have you and Kenneth heard from Kendra?" Keith asked when he called them.

"Well, no, where is she?" Nell asked.

"She went out in this weather and I'm worried about her. I thought she might be over there."

"Why on earth would she venture out on a night like tonight? Kendra isn't that irresponsible."

"Well, Millie got killed and she left in a fixed daze of sorrow, and I don't know where she might be."

"Oh, no, she must be heartbroken. What happened to her little Millie?"

"Millie just had to see what the snow was like. She got out before we could catch her. She ran wild and slammed into some of the back fencing that is covered with snow and broke her neck."

"That doesn't sound like Millie. She never *wanted* to go out. Maybe she wanted to come back over here. Kenneth and I will get in the car and go find Kendra. Kenneth put chains on the tires last night so we can drive on the ice pretty well. Which direction did she go?"

"She headed toward the north. That's the way to the highway so she may be stranded there someplace. I'll get in the truck and come help you."

"Okay, we'll take the south end of the highway, and you take the north end exit and we'll work toward one another to the middle."

Kenneth and Nell were worried as they bundled up and backed down the drive. They didn't know where to start, so before leaving they called the highway patrol and asked for help. Kendra's car, being white would be hard to find.

Before he left the house, Keith grabbed a heavy wool blanket. Something told him he would need it.

~ * ~

Kendra didn't know how long she had walked. The storm was raging and she couldn't see any houses or lights. Her feet were getting numb and she was getting sleepy. *People who are freezing to death always get sleepy* she remembered, so she tried to stay awake. Her hands and wrists had long since lost their feeling and now, out of desperation, she had to force herself to stay awake. She began to sing. The first song that came to her mind was *God Will Take Care of You,* and she began to sing, first softly, then louder and louder. The cold air only hurt her lungs and she had to quit and pull the cap over her face. She didn't know how far she had walked, but she knew that she was not going to find help.

The only thing she could think to do was to go back to the car and at least inside it she would be out of the wind and blinding snow until someone found her.

She turned to go back to the car and the north wind was bitterly cold. Her whole body began to ache and when she finally reached the car, she climbed inside, curled up in a ball, and lulled by the monotonous clicking of the turn signal, fell into an exhausted sleep.

Fifteen

"Oh, Kenneth, whatever do you think happened to Kendra?"

"Now, Nell, let's not borrow worries. Think positive, say a prayer, and we will find her."

Kenneth worked hard to keep the car on the road. Even with chains on the tires, it was slippery and with the snow falling so hard and the wind blowing it, he could barely see out the windshield. And it took the car a long time to warm up enough to be comfortable.

Keith followed close behind them, and turned at the south exit while Kenneth and Nell continued on to exit at the north end. None of the three took their eyes off the sides of the road, looking carefully for any signs of the car or of Kendra.

As Nell and Kenneth edged along the road slowly, all of a sudden, Kenneth saw something he thought looked like the beam of a flashlight.

"Look, Nell!" he cried. "Over there on your side of the road! Do you see a light?"

Nell turned and looked. She took her gloved hand and wiped the fog off the window and sure enough, she saw a faint light.

"Oh, Kenneth, do you think it's the car?"

"We'll just see," he said, and he pulled the car up close and left his headlights burning on bright while he stepped out of the car. He buttoned up his overcoat and stepped deep in the snow as he edged his way to the light. The snow had covered the entire road so he couldn't tell where it dropped off. Very carefully, he felt his way down to the site from where the beam seemed to come. Finally, he came upon the huge mound of snow, under which he found the white car. He cleaned off the snow and before it could cover again, he quickly opened the door.

"Kendra! Kendra! It's Mother and Daddy—can you hear me?" There was no response. Kenneth picked her up and with great effort, accomplished only by the determination that caused the adrenaline to rush, carried her through the deep snow up the embankment and to his waiting car.

The glimpse of her in the beam of the car lights as he walked in front of his car, brought Kenneth Tinker to tears. His beautiful daughter lay limp and unconscious in his arms, not moving or making a sound. He opened the door and placed her inside on the back seat.

"Oh, Kendra, wake up, honey. It's Mother." And tears filled Nell's eyes as she climbed over the front seat to be beside her daughter and try to get her warm. Kenneth glanced in the rearview mirror and saw two cars inching their way toward them. One was the highway patrol; the other was Keith.

When the two cars were close enough, the patrolman got out and talked with Kenneth and Nell. Keith jumped out and ran to the back window and had Nell let it down. He handed her the wool blanket he had brought from home and Nell quickly wrapped Kendra in it. The patrolman got on his radio and called the Emergency Room at Mercy Hospital to be on standby for a possible frostbite victim. Then he escorted them to the hospital, all the while staying in touch with the hospital personnel by radio. Keith got in line and followed close behind.

For the first time since he met Kendra, Keith felt uneasy about their relationship. He broke out in a sweat and beads of perspiration lined his upper lip and his heart raced. As he drove the ten miles-per-hour necessary in the storm, many thoughts went through his head. Would Kendra die? Could he live without her? Would she still love him? Aw, yeah, she'd still love him; he hadn't done anything all that bad, anyway. She just overreacted. She'd get over it and they'd be together again and all would be as it was.

He had convinced himself of this when he drove up behind the two cars at the emergency room entrance. Doctors and nurses were waiting for them and quickly took over. They placed Kendra on a gurney and rushed her inside where a warm whirlpool was waiting. Her feet were in the beginning stages of frostbite, and her hands were swollen and purple.

Her broken wrists needed to be set but that had to wait until her body could warmed up to its proper temperature. Not once did she open her eyes.

"I want to see my wife!" Keith demanded as he walked in.

"Sir, your wife is gravely ill—you will have to wait until we get her out of the woods. Now stand back and let us do our job."

Just for an instant, the caves of blackness in his eyes surfaced, but suddenly receded. But not before Nell noticed it. She remembered seeing that look one other time, and that was when she had first met Keith. She recalled how it had frightened her, but it had been a fleeting moment and she had soon forgotten it. Now she wondered what it all meant.

"Oh, Kenneth," Nell sobbed. "Will she be all right?"

"We will pray, Nell. That's all we can do at this point. Why don't you go down to the hospital chapel? We'll stay here and wait for word."

"Oh, Kenneth, I want to be here when she wakes, so I'll be gone just a little while."

"Now, Keith, I want to tell me what happened?" Kenneth asked, turning toward him as Nell got on the elevator.

Both men sat down on the big divan in the emergency waiting room.

"It's like I told you, Kenneth. She was numb with grief over Millie and took off in the car without thinking. That silly Millie shouldn't have kept trying to get outside and none of this would've happened."

"Kendra has always loved cats—almost as much as her music—so on her sixteenth birthday, I got that kitten for her. I looked a long time for just the right one. It was an absolute thrill for me to watch her face as she opened that little box with the holes in it. I can just imagine how she must have felt when Millie died. If she can possibly come through this ordeal, I will get her another one."

"Well, I might have something to say about *that*!" Keith replied, and the edge to his voice caused a shiver to go through Kenneth.

"Mr. Kouch and Mr. and Mrs. Tinker" came the voice on the speaker interrupting the conversation. "Please come to room five on hall one." Nell came into the waiting room just as the announcement was being made. Together, all three worked their way down to the room where Kendra had been moved.

She lay on the bed, fluids being pumped into her with IV's in each arm, and she was wrapped mummy-style in heavy blankets that had been placed in warming ovens before wrapping her in them. Still, she didn't open her eyes. Keith knelt beside her bed and patted her hand through the thick blankets. He kissed her cheek and brushed her hair back from her eyes. He thought she looked like an angel.

"Baby, I'm here. I'll always be here for you. Don't leave me—I love you so." Kenneth and Nell stood aside while Keith had his moments with his wife. Then they moved over to the bed and Nell whispered to her, "Kendra, you have to get well. Everybody at the school is counting on you. Think of Sarah. She needs you. Now don't give up." Kendra's eyelids quivered a little causing Nell to believe she was listening—*and* hearing!

"Sweetheart, squeeze my hand."

Kenneth felt a slight movement of her hand in his.

"She heard me! She heard me! I know she did!"

"There, there, Mr. Tinker, it is probably just a reflex action—don't get your hopes up too high. The good news, though, is that her body temperature is rising. If it continues at this rate, her temperature could be back to normal in no time. We don't know the extent, however, of her other injuries. We managed to set her wrists, but we had to wait so long, they aren't going to be exactly right. And if she plays the piano as well as you say she does, she may find it won't come easy for her anymore."

Nell's heart sank. Kendra's hands were the very soul and essence of who she was. Her thoughts, beliefs and values were reflected through her music, and gave her life. Tears filled Nell's eyes. Keith got up and put his arms around her trying to reassure her that everything would be all right.

~ * ~

"Mom... Daddy..."

"Kendra! We're *all* here! Keith and Kenneth, she's awake!"

Nell rushed to the edge of the bed. Kendra's eyes were open, but Nell noticed the sorrow there.

Keith went to the other side of the bed as Kendra turned and looked at him. Just as quickly, she turned away as the tears rushed down her cheeks.

"Kendra, we're sorry about Millie. I will try to find you another kitten in due time, but for now, please get some rest. Your mother and I will be leaving to go back home so that your husband can spend time with you alone. We love you, Kendra." And Kenneth bent over and kissed his daughter's damp cheeks.

A look of horror spread over Kendra's pale face and she half rose up from the bed. Terrified, she tried to grab her mother's arm.

"*No*, Mom, you and Daddy stay with me—please," she pleaded.

"Of course, we want to, dear, but Keith has been so worried about you and he helped us find you. I know that you two need to be alone."

"*No!*" Kendra repeated. "*Do not leave me!*" And the horror Nell and Kenneth saw in her eyes troubled them.

"Now sweetheart," Keith replied, "I can stay here with you. Let your parents go on back home. Your good neighbor brought Sammy and the girls and they are in the waiting room now. I'm sure they're anxious to know that you are awake. You are going to be all right, and I won't leave you." And he bent to kiss her.

An automatic reaction, Kendra's arm went up to her face in a protective gesture, shielding herself from his advances.

"Mom, please go tell the girls and Sammy that I'm going to be all right."

Kenneth and Nell had almost forgotten that the children were waiting in the lobby and they knew they'd be anxious to know what was going on. They told Kendra they'd be back and they stepped out to talk to Annanell, Abigail, and Sammy.

"Please come right back," Kendra begged. As they left the room, Kendra turned her face away from Keith's as he moved his chair in closer and began to stroke her hair.

She felt her body go rigid. A rush of complete disgust filled her being as she found that this man, whom she had once loved more than her life, now repulsed her.

"Loosen up, darling, you know how much I love you... You're the best thing to ever happen to me. I only paid Roy Brown to call you because I wanted to see if I could trust you."

Kendra's eyes popped wide. She couldn't believe what she was hearing. As if listening to himself in a room all alone, Keith continued to talk. The sound of his voice droned on and on, and Kendra was crushed and humiliated. Keith didn't seem aware that she was even in the room. As though in a trance, he continued. "I wanted to see how you would act under those circumstances. Only thing is, he kept on calling after the initial deal was done and he was paid. He wanted more money not to tell you. I beat him up pretty good, though, so he won't be calling anymore. Besides, I told him I was going to tell you myself and there would be no need to pay him again."

If Kendra could have, she would have put her hands over her ears. She didn't want to hear anymore. The reality was settling in and destroying all the good memories she had of Keith and their life since they met. All seemed to be coming in crystal clear now as he spoke.

She could no longer ignore his outbursts of temper, and as she thought back, she knew the signs were there, but in her love for Keith, she had chosen to pretend they didn't exist. Now it was too late. Then, as he seemed to come out of a hypnotic trance, Keith focused on Kendra's face. He got right down in her face and told her: "And, honey, as soon as you get well, I'll take you home and we'll begin again. I love you, and I always will."

"I'm sorry, Keith. We could have had it all and now it's gone. All the flowery words and kisses can never erase the hurt and abuse you've caused. I feel sorry for you, Keith, but I can't love you anymore."

"No, no, Kendra—you can't mean that."

"I do mean it, Keith. I wish I could love you again, oh, how I wish I could, but I can't—not ever again."

Kenneth and Nell walked into the room just as Keith laid his head across Kendra's chest and sobbed, his entire body heaving with each gasp. Kendra couldn't feel anything for him at that moment—not even pity. She just wanted him to leave.

Kenneth placed a hand on Keith's back and assured him everything would be all right. He thought Keith's tender-heartedness at that moment needed to be shared with Kendra alone.

"We really need to leave you two together. We'll be back first thing in the morning, Kendra. Dr. Morgan says that you are going to be fine. You may have to practice your piano a lot longer and harder than ever before, though, but therapy will help in relieving the stiffness. And we know you can do it."

"Oh, Mom, I wish you and Daddy would stay with me. Keith is leaving..."

"Oh, no, I'm not. I'm staying with my little lady for as long as it takes."

And he dried his eyes and gave Kendra a kiss.

"You belong to your husband, Kendra. We don't want to interfere with your time together. We'll be back in the morning before you wake up. Good night, precious."

"Okay." Kendra replied weakly. "See you tomorrow."

The nurse came into the room and asked Keith if he would like to have a rollaway bed moved in the room so he could sleep beside his wife. He told her that would be nice. When she returned, she told him that Kendra needed a lot of rest and that he could stay beside her but not to talk to her and keep her awake. Rest was essential for her complete recovery.

Kendra was relieved to hear her say that. The last thing in the world she wanted to do now—*especially now*— was talk to Keith.

She hoped the nurse would give her something to help her sleep because after hearing all that Keith told her, she knew that sleep would never come. As if reading her thoughts, the nurse returned with the bed for Keith and sleeping pills for her.

"Here, dear, you take these to help you sleep."

Kendra gratefully swallowed the tablets and gulped down the water. In just a few minutes, she relaxed and lapsed into the much-needed sleep.

Keith continued to rattle about Roy Brown and how he had betrayed him by continuing to call after he had paid him, and how he ought to be arrested, and how mad he got at him, etc. etc. All through the night he talked, no one hearing him but himself.

Just before dawn, he finally crawled onto the rollaway bed and slept.

Sixteen

Kendra awoke bright and refreshed when the nurse came into her room the next morning.

"Good morning, bright eyes, it's so good to see you better today. We will unhook all your tubes in a little while after the doctor gives the order, and you will be well on the road to recovery. Now I need to take your vitals."

While the nurse hooked up the blood pressure machine, Kendra turned and saw Keith still asleep on the bed next to her and her eyes again filled with tears. She couldn't take her eyes off him as he slept, and she thought of what a waste it was—they had had it all. Now there was nothing. She asked over and over, *What will I do, God? What is Your will for me? Do I stay with this man for the sake of my vows, or do I leave him? Would leaving him help him, or would it cause more damage? Please help me make the right decision, Dear Father; In Jesus' Name, Amen.*

She wanted to discuss everything with her parents, but at the same time, she didn't want them to worry. They would be so disappointed in Keith and they would grieve as much as she had. *Did she want to put them through that?* And yet, if she chose to leave, and she hadn't told them why, they would feel they had failed to teach her the importance of marriage and honoring vows, and they would ask where they went wrong in her upbringing. No, she decided, she would have to tell them. They were her parents and they loved her; they would help her with this heart-rending decision.

Keith opened his eyes, stretched, got up and went to Kendra's side.

"Hello, beautiful, you're looking more like my Kendra now." And he bent and kissed her. He searched through her belongings that Nell brought, and found her hairbrush in the nightstand drawer, and began to brush her hair as it spread across the pillow behind her.

"Keith, I really wish you wouldn't do that." And she turned away from him, avoiding eye contact. She didn't want to ever look into those eyes again and wonder if this was another time for an outburst of temper.

"I want to, honey. You know how much I love you. Remember you're the best thing to ever happen to me."

"No, Keith, I'm *not* the best thing to ever happen to you. If I were, I would have been treasured, as are all good things that come to us. You gave that up, because when you killed Millie, you just finished it and made me realize that I have lived a dream that didn't exist."

And she turned over on her side away from Keith, tears spilling onto her pillow. She knew if she looked at him, she could change her mind. Way deep down in her heart, she had to admit that she would always love him. But she couldn't live that emotional roller-coaster life ever again. To have his love and devotion and kindness one minute, only to lose it the next, and never knowing when it would erupt was beginning to drain her health and she hadn't even realized it. No, she could *never* go back, or *could* she? She would have to trust God to help her with the tremendous burden of making the right decision.

"Won't you give me another chance, Kendra? I promise to control myself. If you had grown up with a father like I had, you may have had this same problem. Don't judge me; stay with me and help me. Remember you promised 'in sickness and health,' and Kendra, *I am sick.* I need you."

Still facing the wall, Kendra wanted to scream. She had no answers yet and needed the time necessary to find them. She wanted Keith to leave the room and give her space to think.

She couldn't think with him in the room and her heart getting in the way. One minute the answers were clear, the next they were muddled. Back and forth, again and again, she struggled with the questions. And no solid answers would come.

"Why don't you go on home, Keith, and start packing up our things? The rent is paid up until the first and that gives us three weeks to get everything out. When they release me, I will go home and help you. But for now, please, just leave."

Keith stood and for a brief moment, his eyes clouded, but with great effort, he pinched his lips together and was able to ward it off for that second. With all the calmness he could muster, he straightened up and gently took her shoulders and turned her over to face him. She had not seen his eyes start to cloud, and the concentration it had taken to maintain his self-control. What she saw at this point was only the gentle brown eyes she had first noticed that evening at the church social when she first met him.

"All right, Kendra. I will go now. I will begin packing our things and I will bury Millie for you. I noticed that you placed her over the tulip bed and I suppose that is where you want to bury her. I will wrap her in your wool muffler that you put across her. I am truly sorry for all the hurt I have caused and I hope you can find it in your heart to forgive me. I believe that God has."

And he walked slowly out of Kendra's room. Even though casts were on her arms, she managed to twist the pillow up around her face, but her muffled sobs could be heard down the hall as he walked out, not looking back.

The nurse brought in Kendra's breakfast tray and removed the rollaway bed as the housekeeping crew came in to clean the room. Soon afterwards, Nell and Kenneth came in with gifts from the people with whom she worked, and also from her church friends. Mr. Fuller and her entire class sent an arrangement of flowers potted in a container shaped like a piano and all had signed the card. Sarah had sent one of her own addressed to "Mrs. Kouch, my favorite teacher in the whole world!" And it was obvious the great effort that had gone into the familiar scrawl. This would be Kendra's most cherished gift.

"Keith gone home?" Kenneth asked as he set the flowers and gifts down on the table.

"Yes, he's gone, and Mom and Daddy, I need to talk to you about some things as soon as I feel up to it."

"Okay, hon, whenever you want to, Daddy and I are ready to listen. Now let me open your gifts for you. It would be hard for you to open them with those casts on your hands. Daddy will feed you while I do this. Sammy and the girls have made you cards and strung beads for a necklace. They are very proud of what they made. The nurse is going to smuggle them in here to see you after a while. They've been so worried about you. Sammy even asked to do the devotional last night so he could specially pray for you, and you know that isn't something Mr. Cool Cat Sammy ever volunteers to do."

Kendra smiled. She hadn't smiled in several days and it felt so good—really good and it caused a sense of relaxation to spread over her being.

Seventeen

Kendra was released from the hospital and she asked Nell if she could go home to recuperate. Nell and Kenneth thought this a strange request, but decided that whatever their daughter wanted to do, she could do it. Her decisions most of her life had been ones to which she had given considerable thought, and she had most always used wisdom in making them.

"You may stay at the house awhile, Kendra. I can help with your therapy while Keith is at work and he can come over in the evenings and I will fix supper for him."

"Oh, Mom, that's what I need to talk to you about. I don't want Keith to come over. I don't want him to be here—ever!"

"Kendra, whatever do you mean? You can't be serious."

"Mom, I *am* serious. There is so much to tell you and Daddy that I don't know where to begin. I need your help."

Kenneth and Nell listened intently as Kendra unraveled the complicated tapestry of her life as she had lived it for the past few months. They sat stunned into silence as

Kendra told them of the physical and verbal abuse to which she had been subjected, and the terrible way Millie had died.

When she had finished and the tears were uncontrollable, Kenneth and Nell held their daughter and wept with her. Realizing something was dreadfully wrong, Sammy and the girls tiptoed into the room and joined with the family to cry and pray together.

"We'll move you home immediately. I'm sorry we didn't know anything about it earlier, Kendra. There is no way that you should've stayed."

"But Daddy, you have always taught us the Scriptures teach that marriage is 'until death separates us' and I can't break that vow so easily. I must think this through and make the right decision—the one God allows me to make."

"We know you will make the right decision concerning this move, Kendra," her mother added. "You need time to think it through."

During the next few days, Kendra gathered up her things and moved home with her parents. It seemed a long time before her casts could be removed and she could get back to her practice. It was going to be like starting over for her. She asked her father to bring her piano home first. The sooner she could get to the practice bench, the better chances for healing to begin. Her fingers protruded from the cast just a few inches, and she tried with all her might to play the piano with the little bit of finger power she had. Her wrists were totally useless. In frustration, many days, she closed the piano cover and placed her head down on the cover, and cried. Then over and over, she returned to try again. She liked to pretend that Millie was there beside her as always, purring her little heart out and waiting her turn "to walk the keys," all the while peering directly into her face with that adorable, inquisitive look.

Back in her old room, she began to try and put the pieces of her life together once again. Nell had left her room intact, and was planning to redo it as a guestroom. Kendra was glad that nothing in it was changed yet.

Keith stayed out of her sight and continued packing things at the house. He took evening rides on his motorcycle, staying until late into the night, coming home just to sleep. At work, his staff wondered how his wife could leave such a handsome, wonderful, caring husband, and they all showered him with sympathy. Keith enjoyed the attention and never admitted to any wrongdoing. He would let Kendra take all of the blame as he glowed with all of the expressions of sympathy and caring.

There was no need to tell them any different. At work he could be what he wanted to be. But at night, in the house alone with his thoughts, he cried himself to sleep every night.

Everywhere he looked, he saw Kendra. Even with all of her things moved out, he could still see and think of her. The fragrance of her Midnight perfume lingered on the bed sheets and pillows, and remnants of her bubble bath and special scented soaps, continually reminded him of what he had lost. The house was hollow without her singing and playing her piano. He was haunted by the memory of her beautiful voice awaking him each morning as she burst into song.

"She'll think this through and come back," he said out loud as he lay across the bed in total darkness.

But it was not to be. Kendra went back to work once the casts were removed and Mr. Fuller and her class greeted her with open arms. Sarah was first in line with the hugs and kisses.

Her classes resumed with all of the enthusiasm they had always had. The students pretended not to notice when they saw how hard and painful it was for her when she played the piano. The tips of her fingers were still slightly numb and her wrists were stiff. She grimaced in pain as she played and the children seemed not to see.

Her first day back on the job, she was called to the telephone. For just a second, her heart jumped, then she remembered that the calls would not be coming anymore.

This time the caller was Keith.

"Please, honey, will you talk to me?"

"Keith, please do not call me at work. Do not call me at home. Do not call me, *period*. Not *now*, not *later*, not *ever*."

"But, Kendra, I need—"

Kendra hung up the phone.

"Poor Dr. Kouch," the women in the school administration office whispered. "He's suffering so much. What kind of woman is Kendra Kouch that she could torture him like this, and he so loving and kind?" And the heads wagged as much as the tongues.

When Kendra found the time and was up to it, she made an appointment to visit with Mr. Fuller. She set the time for after work when he was the least busy.

"Mr. Fuller, I must tell you some things," she began.

"Kendra, if it's about Roy Brown, you will be pleased to know that not only has he been fired, but is awaiting trial for crimes committed against society. He has confessed to not only the calls to you, but to numerous other girls in Brown's Department Store. He has even accused Keith of being an accomplice. Keith may yet be called to be accountable for his actions, too."

Kendra was relieved that Mr. Fuller knew of the calls and that Roy Brown had been caught. She wondered about Judy and how she felt about Roy now. She felt better that now she could close the chapter on that phase of her life. Now she had to deal with what to do. Her head and her heart did constant battle with one another.

Each night she went home to try to deal with what she should do, and she found herself, more than once, questioning God. Back and forth she wrestled with right and wrong, her thinking about the matter and what God's thinking might be on the matter. Always, she came back to the Scriptures and what they had to say.

Heart broken, she appealed to her father. Never in her life had he been unable to answer any question she asked him.

"Daddy, I need help with this decision. I want to do what's right but at the same time, I don't want to live in fear for my life.

"The outbursts were getting closer and closer together and more and more violent. I don't think I can handle the fear of not knowing when one would come. I will become a nervous wreck. Then there's the thought that I know I will always love him. I can think of the good times and a warm feeling covers me and I yearn for those times again.

But the inconsistencies of those times bring on more doubts. What must I do?"

"Come here, Kendra and sit beside me."

Kendra sat down beside her father. Just being next to him gave her a sense of peace. His strength and kindness under pressure and his quiet assurance that all would be all right were what had given Kendra her self-confidence and ability to reason. She loved and respected this man like no other. Nell came into the room just as Kendra sat down.

"Nell, come join us here on the divan. The three of us need to talk. Kendra is having difficulty making this decision all alone. She needs our help."

Nell, with her sweet and gentle nature complemented Kenneth's strength and the two made a perfectly balanced team. Kendra felt complete when the two of them were together.

"Kendra, do you think that God wants one of His children to suffer at the hands of a husband? Do you think the commandment for a husband to 'love his wife as Christ loved the church' is being fulfilled when he mistreats his wife? Do you think that because a woman is a Christian that it gives her husband the 'right' to abuse her knowing that she can't leave him because of her strong beliefs in taking her vows seriously?"

Kendra listened respectfully as her father spoke. Nell kept her arm around her the entire time and gave her a little hug every few minutes.

"But Daddy, there's the promise I made in my vows—I can't break them—can I?"

"When you promised to love Keith in 'sickness and health,' and 'for better or worse,' have you ever thought that to love him during those times may include helping him to change and that the change may only come about if you left? In that sense, you are not breaking your vows. Perhaps he needs a jolt to make him change. Then there is the possibility that he never will. Only time will tell that. But if I were you, I wouldn't worry that God feels you are breaking a vow. Sometimes we have to do what will be the best thing. As parents, we try to do what is best for our children when sometimes it hurts us far more than it does them in correcting them. God corrects His children in the same way. Chastisement often shows love in the deepest sense. And perhaps chastisement is what Keith needs. This is your decision. Do you want to take another chance and have to walk away again, or do you want to do it now and hope for change because of it?"

Kendra felt relieved. "Let me sleep on it, Daddy," she said, and she slowly got up and went upstairs, but not before giving her parents a long, loving hug.

Kenneth turned to Nell and took her into his arms and kissed her. Both felt hot tears on the others' cheek as they held one another for a long, long time.

"How I pray we have raised her right and she doesn't let discouragement set in, Nell."

"Trust her, Kenneth. She is much like you."

Kendra wrestled all night long with her thoughts. She had done this many times but now it seemed more urgent. She was going to have to do something. Now was the time. She must decide soon. Until she could put closure on this part of her life, the wounds opened daily over and over, and it was affecting her work.

She dreamed of the little cabin in Colorado, of the happiest times of her life, of all the good memories and moments with Keith when he had meant the world to her. Did she stop loving him in the bad times and only loved him in the good? What kind of woman was she who could desert a man who needed her? One who needed help? One who really loved her but had a problem? Questions over and over buzzed through her mind and her sleep was restless and filled with turmoil. Would leaving him help him overcome the trouble? Or would it make it worse?

As Kendra lay there in the dark, she listened to the muffled sounds of tears coming from her parents' bedroom. She knew they were feeling her agony and in desperation were trying to come to some helpful terms and words of advice for her. The ordeal had drastically changed the family, but together they were weathering one of life's torrential storms.

They were a family of faith and all decisions ever made concerning their family were based on their close relationship with God. Kenneth had assured her that they would all pull together and get through this as one strong cord of faith.

Kendra turned her damp pillow over and wiped her eyes. She lay in the darkness with her eyes wide open but seeing nothing. How blessed she felt she was to have these two parents. Her father's strength through any crises was the glue that held their family together. And her mother's kind and gentle spirit eased the pain and softened the fear. The thought that she was not alone was a great comfort to her, and pulling the covers around her trembling body, she prayed one final prayer before falling to sleep: *Oh, Dear Heavenly Father, help me make the right decision.*

~ * ~

"Now, honey, don't cry. We'll both be here for Kendra and help her through this. She must make the decision herself—all we can do is give her pointers but then *she* must make *the final* decision."

"Oh, Kenneth, our beautiful, loving daughter should not have to go through this. We don't even have the answers, how can we expect her to have the answers?"

"She *will*, Nell, she *will*. Has she ever failed to weigh all possibilities when faced with a problem in the past? "

"No, Kenneth, she gets her level head from *you*."

"Then we will pray about it and give the burden to God." Holding each other close, Kenneth and Nell prayed together as sleep finally came to them.

Eighteen

Keith tossed and turned in bed. He fluffed the pillow, pounded the bed, and groaned as he cried to himself. He looked at the clock. It was 2:00 a.m. And he still could not sleep. He got up, and went to the garage and rolled out his motorcycle. He didn't bother to put on a helmet or jacket and he was still in his pajamas. The cold wind blew right through him and he didn't even feel it. He raced it as fast as he could make it go and turned the corners leaning so far into it that the foot pedal scraped the ground. The last of the snow was gone and the road was still wet and muddy. But there was one thing he had to do no matter what.

He had to ride down the street where Kendra lived. He made as much noise as he could as he sped along the street. He pulled three good pulls on the throttle in case Kendra was still awake. She would remember what it meant; the three pulls meant 'I love you,' and he wanted to be sure she knew that was still true. Then he sped on down the road to the highway. The bridge had collapsed from the weight of the snow and he didn't see the detour sign that the city had put up. The motorcycle went airborne over the deep cavity underneath it, only to fall about ten feet short of the other side. Keith landed in the muddy ravine and the cycle landed on top of him.

Keith lay there in the wet darkness until the sun came up. He kept going in and out of consciousness. He didn't know how badly he was hurt. He didn't feel anything. He could only think of Kendra.

When the work crew arrived to work on the bridge, they saw the torn up detour sign lying in pieces and the tracks up to the edge of the creek. They hurried down to see how badly the young man was hurt.

The ambulance arrived and took Keith to the same hospital where Kendra had been just a couple of months earlier. In the emergency room, he kept mumbling "Kendra, Kendra, Kendra..."

"Who is he calling?" the emergency room doctor asked. "See if you can contact next of kin."

"Sir, he has no identification on him. He was wearing his pajamas. We don't know who to call."

"Let's see how bad his injuries are for now."

Keith lost consciousness during the examination. Both of his legs and his collarbone were broken. One lung had collapsed and there was internal bleeding. The thing most needed at this point was surgery, and there was no time to waste. When Keith momentarily regained consciousness, he requested that they call Kendra. He was able to tell them the number just before he passed out again.

As soon as Kendra got the call, she rushed to the hospital. From there, she called Edwina and Cal. Kenneth and Nell arrived at the same time. The doctor joined them in the waiting room for Kendra to sign the necessary papers.

"May I see him?" Kendra asked.

"No, ma'am. He has already been prepared for surgery. You may wait in this room and we'll keep you posted." And he turned and walked away.

Cal stared at Kendra with almost hatred in his eyes. Edwina smiled a nervous smile and tried to remain calm. Kenneth and Nell kept a protective arm around their daughter.

"You know this is all your fault, don't you?" an angry Cal asked Kendra.

"Now you wait just a minute, Cal. Kendra cannot take the blame for this."

Kenneth was visibly agitated as he spoke. Nell tried to soften the blow.

"What he means, Cal, is that Kendra did not cause this. Keith brought all of this unhappiness on himself. His temper flare-ups have caused a rip in their marriage that may not ever be repaired. You might ask yourself where he got that awful temper."

Nell couldn't believe she had spoken those words. It was so unlike her to do that, but she was protecting her daughter.

Edwina knew exactly what Nell was talking about and tears filled her big blue eyes. She had lived many, many years in an abusive marriage herself, but for her children's sake, she had remained there. She didn't blame Kendra for a thing. She had been so thankful that Keith had chosen Kendra because she felt her loving disposition might help Keith with his problem, but now she was seeing that even love of the deepest sort couldn't help her son. Nell felt sorry for her. And she realized that she could be seeing what Kendra would be in later years if she chose to stay with Keith. This thought frightened her.

"Well, I would advise you to keep your thoughts to yourself, *Mrs.* Tinker," Cal answered, and his moustache bobbed up and down as he spoke and his dark eyes resembled Keith's at their blackest.

Kenneth opened his mouth to speak, but Nell put a loving hand on his knee and whispered, "It's all right, honey. I'm fine."

All Kendra could do was sob. Seemed to be the only thing she had been doing for the past few months. She was going to have to pull herself together and make a decision one way or another. Her health depended on it.

After a few hours, the doctor came out.

"Keith is very lucky. This could have been fatal. He took quite a fall. He will be all right. It will take time. When he gets out of recovery, we will move him to a room and you can see him then. It will be a couple more hours before we can move him. You may all want to go get a bite to eat."

"I couldn't eat a thing," Kendra said, "But you all go on without me."

Cal and Edwina left, but Kenneth and Nell stayed with Kendra. She curled up on the big leather chair in the waiting room and fell into a debilitated sleep. Somewhere in her subconscious, she could remember hearing three throttle pulls on a motorcycle during the early morning hours but it was like a dream.

"Kendra, wake up. We can see Keith now." Kenneth shook her gently as he spoke.

Kendra got up and together they went to Keith's room. Kendra stood back as his parents went in first. Nell and Kenneth followed. Cal and Edwina went to the bed. Cal took hold of the bed rail and bellowed: "What in the world were you thinking, son? Going out that time of morning without any protection? It's that *woman*, isn't it? Well, maybe you've learned your lesson. And it's about time!"

"Please, Dad, not now... I hurt so much."

"For Pete's sake, Cal, lay off the boy. He's been through enough. Can't you just once, speak kind words?" Edwina's voice broke as she spoke.

"I want Kendra... please get Kendra."

"I'm here, Keith."

Kendra bent over Keith and her heart broke all over again. She couldn't resist and she kissed him tenderly and sincerely on the forehead.

She wanted to take him into her arms and comfort him. He looked so pitiful and helpless lying there in casts and bandages. This feeling was disturbing to her because these thoughts were churning around and around and each minute she thought she had made a decision concerning their life together, something would change her mind.

"I knew you'd come. I know you still love me. I know now that you won't ever leave me." And he closed his eyes.

Kendra pulled up a chair and stayed beside him. Finally, the parents all left so that the two of them could be together. Keith came in and out of consciousness and each time he opened his eyes, Kendra was there. She held his hand and lovingly stroked the top of it, often lifting it to her lips to kiss. Keith smiled.

She studied his every feature as she sat there. She went over and over in her mind all that had happened. She felt that God had given her this quiet time to think things through. Each time Keith opened his eyes, he winked at Kendra and she felt the old feeling return. He reached up and placed his hand on her neck, rubbing it with soft strokes as he told her how he loved her. She felt her body relax and flush warm with desire that only this man could stir, then suddenly she remembered the gush of anger that could erupt at any second, and her body stiffened. She hoped he would go back to sleep. She liked it better when he slept. She could think without interference.

Kendra had been sitting there since the early morning hours and she was tired. She decided to go home and rest so she could go back to work the next day.

Keith held on to her and pulled her to the bedside.

"No! Don't go!" And he pulled her blouse, tearing the seam at the shoulder. "I said *no,* you can't go!" and the familiar look on his face was returning.

Kendra ran out of the room. She would not stay and subject herself to that again. He was never going to change. It would always be that way.

Once in the parking lot, and inside her car, she leaned her head on the steering wheel and cried until there were no more tears.

Nineteen

Kendra returned to work. She was thankful she had her work to keep her mind occupied. Her class was such a blessing to her, each and every one of them. All of them were sympathetic to her inability to play the piano like she once did, and each one encouraged her as much as she encouraged them to learn.

Sarah's adoptive parents were getting up in years and often weren't able to do with Sarah the things younger parents did with their children. Kendra offered to help Sarah with these things and Sarah's mother and daddy were grateful. They wanted to pay Kendra for the extra duty, but Kendra wouldn't hear of it. Every Saturday, Kendra picked up Sarah and they spent time at the zoo, the museum, the art gallery, or attending a concert. This was good diversion for Kendra, also, since she was still indecisive about her marriage. Keith was still in therapy at the hospital and Kendra visited him often although she left her Saturdays open for Sarah. Even with her near blindness, Sarah enjoyed her days with Kendra.

Early on a Saturday morning, as Kendra was preparing to go get Sarah, her phone rang in her room. She listened, horrified, as the voice on the other end told her that Sarah's mother and father had been fatally injured in a wreck at the intersection of Route 66 and Council Road. Sarah's father, an elderly gentleman and her mother had not seen the huge truck barreling toward them as they turned on to the highway, and were hit head on. Their car exploded, and engulfed in flames, it was impossible to reach them. Onlookers just stood helplessly watching the car burn up before help finally came. By the time the fire was extinguished, there was little left.

The voice on the phone was Mark Cannon, lawyer for the McCullough family. "I was instructed to notify you if anything ever happened to Sarah's parents."

"Where is my Sarah?"

"She's here with me. She will need help. She is the only living heir to this family. She is lost with nowhere to turn; she needs you!"

"I'm on my way! Just tell me where to go."

Nell called Kenneth and he rushed home from work to take Kendra over to the lawyer's house. They didn't want Kendra to drive.

When they arrived at the house, Sarah sat in a large, plush chair, trembling and crying. Kendra went immediately to her side.

"Sarah, I'm here. I'll not let anything happen to you and I will help you all I can."

"Oh, Mrs. Kouch, what will I do? Where will I go? What will become of me?"

"Sarah, don't worry about that. We'll take one day at a time and I'll be here for you." Sarah buried her head in

Kendra's arms and sobbed. Mr. Cannon was talking but Kendra was barely listening.

"Kendra, Mr. and Mrs. McCullough left ample provisions for Sarah should anything happen to them. We have learned that they were the anonymous donors who set the music school for talented children in motion. They wanted the very best for Sarah when they adopted her. She will see the finest eye specialists available and will continue with her music. They have requested that you be her teacher and mentor from now on."

Kendra was beside herself with grief for her precious Sarah. She held her until Sarah could cry no more, then asked her to come home with her and her parents.

"You are welcome to stay with us for as long you want, Nell offered.

"Certainly you may be our daughter if you want to be," Kenneth said.

Sarah's wispy blond hair was damp from tears and her dim blue eyes seemed to fade almost completely away in her sorrow. She clung to Kendra as if she feared she would lose *her,* too.

In the days to follow, Kendra helped plan and direct the McCullough's memorial service and stayed close beside Sarah. Little by little, Sarah began to identify more and more with Kendra as a mother figure. She moved her things into Kendra's room for the time being. If Kendra decided she could no longer stay married to Keith, she would be moving to an apartment and Sarah could have her room. If she decided to stay with Keith and try to help him overcome his problem, then Sarah could come to live with them as their daughter. So either way, Sarah would have a place to live.

Mr. Cannon called the Tinkers to his office for a meeting. Nell, Kenneth and Kendra were asked to come.

"I'm going to open the McCullough's will and I need all three of you here to listen to it. This was their request."

Mr. Cannon opened the sealed envelope and began to read:

> *"Let it be known that we, Charles and Marie McCullough, being of sound mind do hereby bequeath all of our worldly possessions to Mr. and Mrs. Kenneth Tinker, to be used for the care and keeping of our daughter, Sarah, and to Kendra, her beloved music teacher and friend. We are confident that all monetary funds left to them will be used for any and all the needs of our daughter. We trust them to fulfill this request. Signed, Charles and Marie McCullough."*

Kenneth and Nell were in shock. Never once had the couple asked them to consider doing this for them. They were flattered and appreciative that someone had that kind of faith in them. They would soon need to consider adopting Sarah for their own daughter. It really wasn't anything they had to think about for long, because they would have wanted to do that even if the will had never been read.

"Maybe I could adopt her," Kendra said aloud. Then, so many thoughts spun through her head. *What if she decided to stay with Keith, and the two of them adopted*

Sarah, would she be subjected to the same abuse from which she had been adopted in the first place? No, she could never take that chance. Maybe if she chose to live alone, she could take Sarah with her. But Sarah needed a father and mother. So maybe it would be best for her to be adopted by her parents and just become another little sister for the four of them. Annanell and Abigail would love it she was sure of it. And Sammy may fuss about being "outnumbered by women!" but in the long run, he would be proud to help Sarah learn the way around the house without bumping into things and stumbling over stuff. And Sarah would have two *parents again!* Then again, she exclaimed outloud: "Yes! That would be marvelous to have another sibling!"

The three of them jumped up and hugged each other. Mr. Cannon was amazed by the love he saw in this family. As a personal family friend of the McCullough's, he had had some misgivings about them writing their will this way, but not anymore. Now he was able to see firsthand the wisdom of such a decision. He should have never doubted the McCulloughs. He smiled to himself thinking how pleased they would be.

It was no time at all until Sarah was safe and secure in the Tinker household. She got up every morning and went to class with her teacher. Everyday she adapted more and more to their home and soon became an important part of it. A sweet child with a loving disposition, she was humble and kind as one who had known much heartache.

Keith was still in therapy at the Jim Thorpe Center in Oklahoma City and continued to improve daily.

He was allowed to go to his office for a few hours a day once or twice a week, but mostly he stayed at the center where they put him through vigorous and difficult routines. He grumbled a lot about it, but he knew it was helping.

At night, he often asked for Kendra, and in the solitude of his room, he cried many tears.

One Sunday afternoon after church, Sarah asked if she could go with Kendra to visit Keith.

"I don't mind, Sarah. I'm sure he needs all visitors he can have. He's one miserable man at this time in his life."

Kendra and Sarah found Keith hard at work on a machine to strengthen his legs when they walked into the therapy room.

Keith was so excited to see Kendra that he lost his balance. For an instant, Kendra wanted to run over and hold him close. But with all her might, she maintained control.

"Hi, honey! Hello there, Sarah. I was sorry to hear about your folks but you couldn't be in better hands than Kendra's."

"Yes, I know, Keith. How are you feeling today?"

"Well, *now,* I'm feeling really well, seeing you two. Come give me a kiss, Kendra."

Kendra just stood still. It took every bit of effort in her body, but she managed to stay put. Instead, she changed the subject.

"Well, you're looking better and you seem to be doing well on that machine."

"My legs are on the mend and we can soon go back home together and start all over, Kendra."

"It would be nice to be that way, Keith."

Sarah and Kendra didn't stay long. Evening services would be starting soon and they didn't want to be late.

"We'll be going, now, Keith. Take care of yourself."

"Yes, do that, Keith, goodbye."

"Hey, you two, don't go. I'll be back to my room soon and we can visit some more."

But Kendra and Sarah were already gone. Keith slammed down the weights on the end of the machine and pounded his fist on the iron rail.

"*Get me outta here—-now!*" he yelled.

Kendra and Sarah could hear him at the end of the hall as they entered the elevator that would take them outside.

"You'll have to trust me and understand, Sarah, for any decision that I may make in the next few weeks. It has been long and hard. I have prayed and agonized over it and although I am still not sure which way to go, I must have your faith and trust in me that I am doing the right thing."

"I do, Mrs. Kouch, I do."

"Sarah, outside the classroom, you may call me 'Kendra.' After all, we *are* sisters, you know."

Sarah beamed.

"Kendra Kouch! How in the world are you? I've missed you so much."

Sarah looked up to see Judy McClure walking toward her.

"Judy! How nice to see you. Are you still working for Brown's?"

"No, Kendra. After I heard what that lousy Roy Brown did to you, I quit. I hope he gets what he deserves. I am so sorry that happened to you. I'm working at JC Penney's now and I like it all right.

"My husband and I have reconciled and I think that maybe we may make it this time. Because of your influence, we decided to try and find purpose for our lives. We decided that maybe we had missed the whole point of everything. We found it just where you once told me to find it, and that's in the Lord. I have wanted to thank you for showing me the way." And she gave Kendra a big hug.

Kendra felt ashamed that she had helped someone else while she was helpless to help her own marriage, which was falling apart. This caused her to again reconsider her decision. When was this going to end? What could she decide that was right?

"And who is this lovely child?" Judy asked.

"Judy, this is my new little sister, Sarah. She is one of my students at the Kerr Music School for the Exceptionally Talented Child. She is a true genius when it comes to music. You'll have to come to our next recital. She'll shock and amaze you with her ability."

Sarah blushed.

The two women hugged goodbye and Sarah and Kendra went to the car. They made it back just in time for evening church services. Kenneth and Nell were beginning to worry about them, but they came into the auditorium just as the first hymn was announced. Nell was glad they made it because she had a surprise for Kendra.

"Come here, Kendra. Someone is here to see you," Nell told her after church was over.

Kendra saw a young man walking toward her smiling a broad smile. He walked with a familiar gait and a confident air about him, but Kendra couldn't think who he could be. The curly brown hair and green eyes seemed to strike something in her memory, but she couldn't put a finger on it. As he got closer and closer, her mind whirled about with questions. Just as he got almost to her, she squealed, "Tom! Tom Baker! What in the world are you doing here?" And she didn't try to hide her joy at seeing him.

"Hi, half-pint!" And he picked her up and swung her around like she was as light as a cloud.

"Home on leave for a few days and thought I'd come see my favorite little girl!"

Tom Baker was the son of Nell's dearest friend, Joyce Baker. Joyce's daughter, Eileen was Kendra's best friend. They had grown up together and Tom, being the older brother always considered the two girls a couple of pests. If they were outside playing together, and Tom came home, he might just as well give up. They followed him everywhere he went and he had not a moment's peace. Joyce and Nell often laughed as they agreed he probably joined the Marines to get away from the two girls. Kendra lost touch in the years to follow and had not seen him since she had grown up.

"My, my, my, what time does do for a little girl! She becomes a woman! And a beautiful one at that," Tom exclaimed as he set her down.

"Oh, Tom, Eileen and I were such messes. I hope you got over it! I just thought you were so handsome and Eileen was so proud you were her brother. It's good to see you again."

"Yeah, you too. I would have known that golden red hair anywhere—no one ever had hair like Kendra Tinker. Well, good to see you again—maybe we can get Eileen and all go to supper one night before I have to leave. Mom says she scarcely comes around anymore, now that she's married."

"Well, I'll get her and we'll all go to supper one night soon. Goodbye."

"Oh, Mom, thanks. That brought back a lot of memories. I'm so glad and thankful for Joyce and Eileen. They were always such good friends."

"Yes, Joyce was the best friend I ever had. I miss her still today."

Joyce had died from cancer just after Kenneth and Nell had celebrated their twenty-fifth wedding anniversary, and Nell could still feel the void. Joyce's husband had remarried and moved out of state. Although Eileen and Kendra stayed in touch, Tom had not. Kendra was pleased to have enjoyed a moment from the past—a happy moment.

Kendra went home and opened her piano. She sat down and began to play.

She played as best she could with her numb fingers and weak wrists, but she could tell there was a slight improvement. Sarah sat beside her and they played a duet and sang together. Kendra messed Sarah up a time or two, but Sarah didn't seem to notice. She just went on with the piece as though nothing happened. It was often discouraging to Kendra, but she kept trying and trying.

That night, Sarah and Kendra talked about their physical problems.

"You know, Kendra, you could be my eyes, and I could be your hands. Together we would make a real team."

Kendra respected and admired Sarah's wisdom and maturity for one so young. They began to spend evenings dreaming up a routine that they could do together that would be both fun and entertaining. All of these things were pleasant diversions for Kendra, but they were also keeping her from deciding what she had to decide. Keith would soon be going home from the hospital and expecting her to be there with everything moved back in for them to begin all over. Could she do that?

The next evening Kendra slipped out to go for a drive. She was going out to the Botanical Gardens for a while by herself. She needed a place to be alone and to think things through without distractions of little sisters and a brother." I'll be home after a while!" she whispered to her mother as she went out the door.

She drove straight to the park and walked over to the pond where she and Keith had spent their first date. She looked for the two beautiful swans they had admired that day. She hoped their serene peacefulness would be tranquil therapy for her, so she was very disappointed when she did not see them. With spring still a few weeks away, she felt slightly chilled as she buttoned up her sweater to the neck. Sadly, she sat beside the water and thought about all that had happened. She would have to make up her mind soon. Time was running out.

She pulled her knees under her chin, put her head on her knees and kept her eyes shut. She wrapped her arms around her knees, and in desperation, prayed.

"Dear God, please give me an answer. I want to do Your will. I want to be happy, but I also want happiness for Keith. I want to help him; I love him so much. Give me courage to abide by a decision that is right. In Jesus' Name, Amen."

She didn't know how long she had been sitting there, when she felt a tug at her sweater sleeve.

"Ma'am, you need to go now. It's getting late and you shouldn't be here by yourself. We just don't know what kinds of folks come around here after dark, so you best get home."

Kendra opened her eyes to see the security guard standing over her.

"We used to have a pair of swans on the pond, but someone came in and killed the male. We found him on the grass with a broken neck."

"You know, swans mate for life, and the female searched and searched and grieved, but was finally able to fly away and make it on her own. We still don't know who killed the swan, but someone who would do that may do cruel things to people, too, so you better run on home now."

Kendra thanked the man and returned to her car.

She sat there a while longer thinking. Had God given her a sign? And if so, how should she interpret it?

"Dear Father, were you giving me a sign? How am I to read it? That I have picked a mate for life and I must stay, or that as a hurt mate, I can 'fly away' and make it on my own?"

Back to square one, Kendra headed home. Shadows of the early evening were beginning to fall and as an afterthought, she suddenly made a sharp turn toward a different direction. She had to go by the house that she and Keith had rented when they married. As she turned into the drive, her eyes filled with more tears.

A rush of memories, both sweet and bitter flooded her being and she was overcome with sadness. The curtains gone, the house empty, she looked into its windows and it *looked* as forlorn as *she* felt. Cal and Edwina had cleaned out all of Keith's things when he went to the hospital, and her things had been moved out long before that.

Kendra walked around to the back yard. Next to the patio was the little grave in the flowerbed where her precious pet lay. Tiny shoots from the Tulip bulbs were pushing their way through the small mound of dirt, giving Kendra a sense of peace, even within the sorrow she felt. She stood a long time at the little grave, and thought of her little friend and the joy that having a pet brings. After a lot of thought, she wandered back to her car. Slowly she backed out, and began the drive back home as the darkness of the evening surrounded her.

"Where were you, sweetheart? Daddy and I were worried about you." Nell looked up from making supper as Kendra came into the kitchen.

"Oh, Mom, I just had to revisit our little home one more time. I just wish I knew what was the right thing to do. I have bounced back and forth again and again, still no answers come."

"They will come, Kendra, they will come. But for right now, your father wants to see you in his study."

Kendra slowly opened the door to the study where Kenneth sat in his recliner.

"Come over here, Kendra. I have something for you."

He handed Kendra a little box with holes punched in it and tied with a blue satin ribbon, much like the one he had given her on her sixteenth birthday. Her heart leaped with joy! *Can it be?* she thought. *She hoped*! Quickly, she untied the blue ribbon and there, peering at her with round, innocent, trusting eyes, was a beautiful, blue-eyed Persian kitten!

"Oh, you darling little dumpling!" And she picked up the wide-eyed kitten and cuddled her in her arms, the kitten purring contentedly.

"That's your name, '*Dumpling*,'" and the kitten sniffed Kendra's nose. "Oh, Daddy, thank you, thank you!" And she fell to her knees beside his chair and threw her arms around his neck, Dumpling wedged between them.

It had been sometime since he'd seen his daughter sparkle with happiness and it did his heart good. Kenneth Tinker smiled.

Twenty

Oklahoma spring weather came in full force in the next few weeks and tornado warnings were issued from the weather service almost nightly. One of the first things that Kenneth Tinker did for his family was to build a house with a basement when they moved to Oklahoma and their children were small. They were one of the lucky families because not all Oklahomans shared the fear of tornadoes that Ken Tinker did.

As a child he had been caught up in one of the worst storms in Oklahoma history and he had never forgotten it. His father and his brother were killed in that storm and he vowed that he would always have a storm shelter or a basement. During the tornado season in Oklahoma, Kenneth Tinker would be found in his study listening to the weather reports. At the slightest hint of a high wind, the family would draw together in the basement to sleep out the night.

The night of the big storm, the family, complete with Dumpling, was gathered in the basement when the news over the radio reported that a tornado had all but wiped out a section of Oklahoma City. Terrified, Kendra feared for Keith's parents. As the news continued, their worst fears were realized. It had hit hardest the very addition in which Cal and Edwina Kouch lived. Power lines down, phones out and flooding everywhere, it was impossible to know if they were even alive.

At the hospital, Keith was sick with worry. No one could find out any information and it may take days to find out anything. Keith could not call out and no one could call in. The City was in complete chaos, and Keith was at a breaking point. He had a severe relapse when the word finally reached him. He was returned to his wheel chair for safety's sake and given strong sedatives to calm him.

Morning came and the destruction was devastating. How anyone could have lived through it was to be a miracle. The TV cameras scanned the area and there were flattened houses with nothing but foundations remaining, cars at the top of trees, and "live" power lines strung all across the streets and sidewalks. South Oklahoma City had the look of a war zone, and the damage was estimated in the millions and millions.

The Red Cross notified Keith's brother, Kyle, serving the military in Germany, and Kayla learned of it through the Red Cross in Arkansas where she lived. It was true; Cal had lost his life and Edwina was critically injured. Ironically, she ended up in the same hospital where Keith and Kendra had been a few months beforehand. As soon as roads were opened, Kendra rushed to her mother-in-law's side.

In ICU, Kendra could only visit her once every four hours, then for only a few minutes. Edwina and Cal were coming in from the grocery store when the storm hit. The wind caught Cal and jerked him upwards of fifty feet and slammed him with full force into the side of the brick fence surrounding the gated community where they lived, killing him instantly. Edwina almost made it to the cellar when the door was blown off as she opened it, injuring her when it fell on top of her.

"Can you hear me, Edwina? It's Kendra." There was no answer. Edwina was in a coma.

Kendra bent low and kissed the woman on the cheek and brushed her hair back from her face.

Just as soon as Kyle could get a leave, he hopped a plane straight home and Kayla along with her husband and new baby arrived shortly afterward. Keith felt helpless and alone at the Rehabilitation Center where he was continuing his therapy. The rage within him was building and there was no one there to calm him.

With Kendra spending time with his mother, his loneliness was overwhelming and he became depressed as well as angry.

When all gathered in Edwina's room, it was decided not to tell her of Cal's death until she was well enough to understand it. This may mean that she would not get to attend the funeral. It may mean that she would *never* understand it.

"With no home, you will all need a place to stay. We have plenty of room at our house and my parents would be glad to put you up for as long as you need to stay," Kendra reassured the grief stricken family.

When the group got back to the Tinker house, Nell and Kenneth welcomed them with open arms and a good home-cooked supper. Nell had prepared the basement apartment for them with clean linens and plenty of food in the recreation room kitchen. She had even crawled up into the attic and retrieved her children's crib so that Kayla's baby would have a place to sleep. Everything was made for their comfort as they went about the sorrow of preparing for a funeral, keeping watch over their mother, and keeping Keith calm all at the same time. Kendra was running her legs off trying to see to all of their needs. She asked Mr. Fuller for a short leave of absence at her job to take care of the needs of everyone. She told Mr. Fuller that Sarah would be a perfect substitute for her and to utilize her talents all he could. The experience would be priceless for her. There would be so much to do. She couldn't think of work at this time. With everything that belonged to the Kouch family gone; there were no insurance papers, no records of any kind, not even a photo, a scrapbook—no memories at all of the family. News reports were saying that people as far away as Kansas were picking up rain drenched photos and gathering them in sacks to return to Oklahoma City so that families could look through them. The winds had scattered belongings and pictures for miles and miles.

As Kendra leafed through the entire assortment of papers on the table at the community center, she found a torn and tattered family Bible. She opened it carefully and read the inscription, even though the dampness had caused the ink to run. It said: "To Edwina and Cal Kouch—may the words in this book be ever near and dear to your hearts. Love from your children—Christmas 1945." She gingerly picked up the pieces as they hung from the binding, and placed it in a plastic bag to bring home.

"Don't you even care my father is gone?" Keith sobbed to a grieving Kendra when she entered his room. "And that my mom is critical?"

"That's not fair, Keith. You know that I'm sorry for you and your family. Cal was a man of many faces, but I'm sure that in his own way, he loved you as he did the twins."

"Yeah, right! He loved me like a person loves a snake."

"And your mother adores you, Keith, you know that she does."

Kendra felt her heart melt at the sight of this pitiful man who couldn't express his love for his father in the same way his father could never express *his* love to *him*. She moved toward Keith and placed her arms around his neck. Still in his wheelchair, he pulled her down and kissed her. For one brief moment, she was his again, loving and happy as it had been in the beginning. And for one succinct moment, Kendra erased from her mind all that had transpired, and the tenderness of his embrace brought a surge of desire that this man had always been able to awaken in her.

Quickly, she regained her composure and gently pushed Keith away. *I cannot think of ever letting this happen again,* she thought. She quietly left his room as he dissolved into tears that she could hear all the way down the hall.

Kendra joined in to help the twins with funeral services, offering to sing the songs that Cal and Edwina loved. All of them together planned the service and it was to be held in the church they all attended. Doctors said Keith could go to the service, but only in his wheelchair and only for a short time. Kendra's heart began to once again soften toward him. She was so sure that she had made the right decision and now this.

The never-ending seesaw of emotions was beginning to tell on her and she would burst into tears at the drop of a feather. It was a good thing that she wasn't going to work for a few weeks; she wouldn't be able to function properly.

The funeral was well attended by the friends at the church they had attended since moving to Oklahoma City. Kendra's best friend, Eileen came to offer her moral support and her brother Tom came with her. Eileen saved a seat for Kendra by the two of them so that she could join them when she finished her solo, *It is Well With My Soul.* Kyle pushed Keith's wheelchair as Kayla and her husband, carrying the baby, walked behind. Edwina was still in a coma and sadly, could not attend her husband's funeral.

After Kendra's solo, she stepped down from the platform and took her seat beside Tom and Eileen. Her father sat on the other side of her and her mother next to him. Annanell and Abigail, along with Sammy and Sarah, sat on the other end of the row. Kendra glanced up to see Keith staring at her, the deep dark blackness of his eyes slowly rising and she feared what was about to happen. How often had she seen that sign and how often had she seen what would follow. She fidgeted as the minister continued the eulogy, and glancing over she could see Keith's knuckles turning white as he gripped the arms of the wheelchair harder and harder. Sweat was breaking out on his upper lip, the veins were standing out on his neck—the signs she knew too well—and he raised himself up out of the chair, and stumbled across the isle and grabbed Tom by his necktie.

"What are you doing sitting by my wife?" he yelled. A startled Tom stood and tried to calm the angry young man as Kyle and a few men of the church subdued Keith, placed him back into the chair, and rolled him out to the lobby where all could still hear his screaming and anger. Kendra brushed aside the tears and tried to concentrate on the service. In the background, she heard the screams get further and further away as one of the funeral attendants took Keith back to the rehab center after medics were called and he was sedated. Kendra hoped they would keep him that way for a few days longer.

"I'm so sorry, Tom. Keith is going through a difficult time now. I hope you can forgive him."

"It's all right, Kendra. It's not your fault. I just hope that *you* are all right."

They went out to get in the line for the trip to the cemetery. No one spoke. Nell and Kenneth held hands quietly, tears sparkling in the corners of their eyes.

"I want all of you, friends and relatives alike, to come to the house for supper before you leave," Nell said to the family members present as they stood around the grave.

"After supper, we will all go to the hospital and it will be about time for the doors to the ICU area to be unlocked for your visits. We will be able to console Keith, too."

The Rehabilitation Center chose to dismiss Keith and re-admit him to the hospital that had sent him to them. It was decided that he needed psychiatric attention as well as medical treatment. They would resume the therapy treatments just as soon as Keith was mentally able to handle them. The only blessing in this move was that now he was in the same hospital with his mother, and maybe this could prove tranquil for him and help him in his recovery. His breakdown was a combination of it all, his father's death, his mother's critical condition, his seeming inability to control himself, and the loss of Kendra.

Visiting hours were just beginning when the group arrived at the hospital. Edwina was responding to tests and seemed to be coming out of her coma. As she began to stir, the nurse went to Keith's room and rolled him down so that he too, could be there when she awoke. Calm by now, Keith with his two siblings stood by their mother's bed awaiting anxiously as she began to make noises and her eyelids began to flutter. When they opened wide, it was so good for them see those big blue eyes again, and they surrounded her with hugs and kisses.

Now the time had come to tell her about Cal. Each one dreaded to be the one to tell her.

"Mom..." Kyle began.

"Don't say anymore, Kyle. I know that your father is gone. You don't need to tell me anything else. It was like a dream, but I saw him hit the brick wall and knew that he had not survived."

And looking at Keith, she held out her hand to him, "And Keith, your father loved you. It was hard for him to express the deepest feelings and his military training was one that to you seemed harsh and improper. But he had his good points; he was a hard worker and I learned to overlook his fits of temper and often made him laugh at himself. It wasn't always easy, but with hard work and patience, it worked for me."

And all of them joined their mother as she burst into tears.

The words hit Kendra like a dart. Were they meant *for her?* She wasn't as strong as Edwina and she didn't know how she could possibly endure anymore of Keith's outbursts, but if she loved him as Edwina had loved Cal, she *could—couldn't she?* She quietly walked out unseen and met Nell and Kenneth in the lobby to wait. Again, she was on her merry-go-round. What *must* she *do?*

The family, with arms entwined left the hospital to go home. In silence they drove into the drive and in silence, they walked into the house. Dumpling was waiting patiently—like Millie used to do—for Kendra to get home. There was a big difference in Dumpling and Millie, though, and Kendra had learned it right from the start. When she called Dumpling, she wouldn't come. She bumped into walls and sudden noises did not scare her. She was seemingly calm and unruffled when anything happened out of the ordinary. Kayla's baby could cry and squeal and Dumpling remained tranquil and calm. Finally, Kendra realized that little Dumpling was deaf! For this reason, Dumpling demanded a lot of understanding and care. And this was good for Kendra during this traumatic time in her life. The kitten gave her other things to think about as she protected her from all hurt and fear. The two bonded instantly.

Exhausted from the day's activities, Kendra announced she was going upstairs to bed. "I'll have the nightly devotion with the children in my room, Mom. You coming, Sarah? Come on, Sammy, and girls," and she picked up the purring Dumpling and cuddled her as she climbed the stairs to her room. The other children followed her close behind.

Nell and Kenneth unwound in the study and were trying to relax when they heard the car turn in. Kayla came in and put the baby to bed, then they sat down to decide what to do next. Kyle suggested that when his mom was released from the hospital that they rent a place for her and Keith to live. Another thought was that maybe she could go home to Arkansas with Kayla and her family. But where would that leave Keith? No doubt he would have some recuperating to do and need some help.

"I don't know what all has transpired between Keith and Kendra," Kyle said, "But I do know my brother—his temperament is much like Dad's. He struggles with this daily, and there will be few people who can handle his personality. I was thinking that maybe we go back and rent that house he and Kendra rented and move him and Mom into it. The flowerbeds were already started, the lawn had been sodded, and the house had been painted and it is perfect. They still have some rent paid up on it, too. I think Keith would like that idea."

Nell and Kenneth sat silently by, and just listened. Their daughter had also been through a hard time, and they wanted what was best for her, too. Should she decide to stay with Keith, maybe Edwina being there for a time until she could get on her feet would be a good thing. *Maybe not.* And maybe Kendra would decide *not* to go back to Keith—*ever.* In any case, the house would have to be completely refurnished. Everything Cal and Edwina had had was gone. Edwina would be starting all over.

Everybody said their goodnights and went their different directions to bed. It had been a totally devastating and draining last few days. Sleep was a welcomed commodity.

175

Twenty-one

Kyle got up early to go to the hospital to visit with his mother and Keith about the possibilities they had discussed with other family members after the funeral. He walked into ICU after pushing the button that opened the door, and found his mother sitting up in bed, sipping a cup of hot tea.

"Mom, you look wonderful! Just as soon as the stitches are out of your head, the dizziness is gone, and all danger of seizures are gone, you get to go home."

"Home? Son, I have no home. I am totally without home or belongings. I am an orphan in the most honest sense." Strong woman that Edwina Kouch was, the tears still poured. Just as quickly, she regained her composure and reached out to hug her son.

The next few minutes were taken up telling Edwina of the decision she would need to make.

"I think the idea of renting the house out in the country is the best idea of all."

"I'll visit with Keith about the idea and if he okays it, I will stay as long as it takes to refurnish the house and get it ready for you and Keith to occupy it. I won't leave you until we get you on your feet and up and running again. Kayla will probably stay, too although her husband may have to go back if it takes too long. The Tinkers have generously taken us into their home until we can get things settled."

"They are a wonderful family and generous and kind. Kendra comes by her kind nature naturally. You may want to go up to Keith's room and tell him of the plans. We must not leave him out, son."

Kyle left the ICU ward and rode the elevator up to Keith's room. He was sitting by the window looking out at the near-spring day that was beginning. He was thinking of how he had met Kendra in the spring and what all she had meant to him. He was thinking that he really botched up a perfect match and *what is wrong with me?* He asked himself that question over and over. No answers came. He turned as Kyle walked into the room.

Kyle pulled up a chair and the two talked for a few hours about everything: Their childhoods, their differences, their similarities, their mutual love for their mother, and their mutual distrust of their father. It was longer than the two boys had ever talked. Keith was unusually calm and his gentle nature shone through as never before. He apologized for the outbreak in the service, and he told Kyle the story of Kendra and losing her. He begged forgiveness for all of the things of the past, and the two brothers, for the first time in their lives, "found each other."

"I *like* the idea of renting the house. Let's *do* it."

"Then it's settled."

The weeks to follow were spent in doing up the rent house, getting it ready for Edwina and Keith at such time as they would be dismissed from the hospital. Edwina was moved to a room and Keith spent a lot of hours in her room talking to her about his troubling nature and what he could do to correct it. She was a good friend and mentor. Nell and Kenneth were both frequent visitors to see her and that friendship blossomed and grew.

Soon it was time for Keith to return to therapy and take up where he left off. It wasn't long until he was back on the irons and pumping them in an effort to build back up what he had lost. His legs were returning to normal, slowly but surely, and his vigor was building daily. And still his thoughts were of Kendra day after day after day.

It looked like Edwina was going to be released before Keith, so the day that she was to check out, the whole crew went to get her.

Nell and Kenneth took her to their home and she stayed there for several days to get her strength back to normal, then they took her over to look at her "new" house.

Kyle and Kayla had spent time and money getting it fixed up to look as much like the old home as possible. They shopped all over Oklahoma City trying to reproduce furniture pieces like they had, and they tried to duplicate the atmosphere so that Edwina would feel right at home. Nell even bought material and made the same curtains all over again for sixteen windows!

When Edwina got out of the car and they led her carefully into the door, she gasped. Her eyes filled with tears, and she hugged herself and turned around and around.

"It's beautiful!" was all she could manage to say.

Soon she was moved in and she had two of her children and a grandchild to keep her company and help her until she was strong and until Keith could come home. Nell and Kenneth began to miss them, and also began to miss having a baby around the house. Their house was eerily quiet, even with four little children and a grown daughter in it. Nell called every day to check on Edwina. Things were slowly getting back to normal for them.

As Kendra was preparing to go see Keith one morning, she began to think of all the events leading up to where she was now and she honestly had to admit she was getting to where she was anxious to see him. She was beginning to re-evaluate what she ought to do. He was unusually self-controlled and it was like meeting him for the first time all over again. She found herself putting on her prettiest clothes to go see him and she began to dream of, and look forward to, his kisses. His physical therapy as well as the mental therapy seemed to be working. She picked up Dumpling and hugged her as she checked her closet for just the "right" thing to wear. She even began to sing again—she felt she had almost lost the ability. The kitten looked up at her with adoring eyes.

Keith's office remembered him almost daily by showering him with gifts and cards. He seemed happier and more content and Kendra hadn't seen the darkness rise in his eyes since the funeral. She dressed in the peach blouse that she first wore with Keith and added the copper colored skirt.

"I'm going to check on Keith, Mom—I'll be back in time for supper!"

"Okay, honey, I'm going to check on Edwina and take a pot of stew over for their supper, but I'll be here when you get back."

Kendra peeked into Keith's room and he was asleep. She tiptoed over beside his bed and just watched him snooze. My, how handsome he was. She wanted to touch him, cuddle him and run her hands through his thick, black hair. Just as she leaned down to kiss him, he awoke and grabbed her, pulling her down beside him.

"I'm *so* glad you came, Kendra. I love you so much and I am so sorry for the horrible way I acted at the funeral. Can you ever forgive me?"

"Keith, we've been all through this. You know that you're forgiven."

"Give me a kiss, sweetheart," and Kendra melted once again into the strong arms that she so wanted to never leave.

"Your mother really likes the house. She will be happy there and hopefully, you will be company for one another after Kyle and Kayla and the baby leave."

"You'll come home to me over there, too, won't you, Kendra?"

"Keith, I am torn through all of this. I want so badly for us to be together again, but I have to wait and see..." her voice trailed off and she turned to gaze out the window. She did not see the rise of blackness in Keith's eyes as he mustered ever bit of control he could to fight off the anger building inside him. As Kendra turned, the deep rage had subsided and she had not seen it.

"Let's give ourselves more time and not rush it, Keith. We'll see."

"Whatever you say, baby..."

Kendra told Keith goodbye and left the hospital just as the giant orange ball was disappearing over the horizon. All the way home, she was lost in thought. The problem was even greater now and the decision even more difficult. Was she setting herself up just to endure the same hurt all over again?

Since Dumpling couldn't hear when Kendra came in, she just parked herself by the door and waited. Sometimes Kendra stumbled over her since she didn't hear her and know to move. Kendra looked behind the door as she slowly opened it, and scooped Dumpling up and the kitten purred. What a joy she was to Kendra and how she eased the pain of the problem facing her. Kendra cupped Dumpling's little face in her hands and "told" her by touch how very much she loved her. The kitten seemed to always read Kendra's mind and she closed her eyes and purred.

Nell was in the kitchen and supper was ready when Kendra came through the utility room into the kitchen.

"How was Edwina today, Mom?"

"She was much better. She is dreading it when the twins have to leave. But she's looking forward to Keith coming there to be with her and help her. Do you have any idea how much longer Keith will be in therapy?"

"I think he has a ways to go yet, Mom. Some days he has setbacks and has to start over, but now that his attitude is better, they say that's half the battle."

"I've noticed a change in you, Kendra. Your father has noticed it, too. Are you thinking of changing your decision, or had you ever really completely decided on what to do?"

"Oh, Mom—I do love him so much. I want to be with him the rest of my life. But what if it all starts again? I can't run back and forth and back and forth; I will be a mental case and my health will not stand it. All of this has been hard enough as it is. I do see a change in him, though, and maybe it would never happen again—I just don't know."

"Well, take your time. Don't make any rash decisions. Let time tell what he has become."

"I will, Mom, but oh, how much I miss him."

Soon it was time for Kendra to return to work. She was glad to see her class again and the progress they had made in her absence. Sarah had done an excellent job filling in for her and she had proudly told all the students that "Now I am Mrs. Kouch's sister!"

Kendra greeted each student with a hug and they began to get down to business. As she sat on the piano bench, a phone call for her was announced on the intercom. Excusing herself she went into Mr. Fuller's office. He was beaming as he handed her the phone.

"Hello, this is Kendra Kouch."

"Yes, Mrs. Kouch. This is Dr. Jon S. Thornton in Germany. I am an eye surgeon, and although we have never met, I feel that I know you and know you well. Sarah's mother and father told me about you a long time ago when they contacted me to consider Sarah's eyes and if there was anything that could be done to stop her pending blindness. They set up funds and put their name in for such time that I would have an opening for her case.

Well, I have set up a time if you are in a position to accompany her here."

Kendra's mouth flopped open and she turned and tossed Mr. Fuller a questioning look. He was smiling and nodding an enthusiastic "*Yes!*"

Kendra turned back and with all the excitement in her voice of a small child anticipating a trip to Disneyland, she responded with, "Yes! I am!"

"Then I will expect you in two weeks. My staff will meet the two of you and we will begin. Good luck, and our team will do the best we can for your little Sarah, whom I just learned is now your little sister!"

"Yes , she sure is—my little sister! Thank you, Dr. Thornton!"

"Well, honey, you can thank Sarah's parents. They planned long and hard for this dream and I intend to do my best. See you in two weeks!"

Kendra was so excited that she could barely tell Sarah the news. She asked the class for their undivided attention while she made an announcement. All the instruments that were being tuned suddenly grew still and the children sat in respectful silence while Mrs. Kouch relayed the message to them. The children burst into applause and cheers and it went on for several minutes before Kendra could restore order. Then they crowded around Sarah and hugged her and wished her well. Sarah's smile was as broad as a canyon.

Kendra could hardly wait to tell Keith the news. She hurried to the hospital after work to tell him. As she came down the hall, she could hear him talking to the nurses as he was working out on the machines in the physical therapy wing of the hospital. The noise from the weights and the whirling sounds of the machines almost drowned out the music that was being piped into the room. But even above all the noise, she could hear Keith.

"Get your hands off me! I can do this by myself! You big ape, stop it! I don't need you or anyone else to help me! Stop treating me like I'm helpless!"

Just at that moment, Keith looked up to see Kendra standing in the hall about to turn away and go back home.

"Hey, beautiful! Don't leave! Come on in! I'm so glad to see you!" And he held out his arms expecting her to run into them. She did not.

Very slowly, Kendra walked over to his side. He slipped his arm around her waist and pulled her close. The nurses backed away and walked from the room, their eyes round with fright.

"I *knew* you'd come today—*I just knew it*!"

"I think I may have come at a bad time, Keith."

"No, there is no 'bad time' for *you, Kendra,*" and he leaned down and kissed her long and hard on the lips. Kendra felt the weakness in her knees, the feeling that she had felt so often long ago that could make her deny all reasoning and logic, and send her, magically, to another dimension in time and space. She almost forgot what she came to tell him, and soon the temper she had just witnessed seemed unimportant. Was it even anything to be concerned about?

"Keith, I'm taking Sarah to Germany. Dr. Thornton called today, the world-famous eye surgeon, and he has scheduled an appointment for her. He thinks there may be hope for either curing or stopping the trauma that is slowly stealing her sight! Isn't that wonderful? I couldn't wait to tell you!"

"That means I won't see you for *four weeks?*" And the pressure began to mount.

"Stop Keith! Stop this instant! Calm down! Yes, I will be gone about four weeks, but just think, Sarah may be able to see when we get back!"

"Sarah, Para, I don't give a care about Sarah, I just want you!"

Kendra's eyes began to mist. She was so disappointed. She thought Keith would be as excited as she was about the appointment. She could see now that Sarah meant nothing to him, only his selfish, hateful self, meant anything at all. She decided then and there that she would go to Germany in two weeks and would not return to see him until she was back. He could just cool off and think about how hateful he can be while she was gone.

She turned to leave and once again, Keith turned on the charm.

"I'm sorry, baby. Kiss me."

But Kendra was already out the door.

"I'll see you when we get back!"

"Well, I may be gone home when you get back!" Kendra did not hear that. She was far down the hall and gone.

Twenty-two

Germany was a gorgeous country! Kyle was stationed there and had sent his brother many pictures, but Kendra did not think any of the photos that Kyle had sent them did the country justice. She described its incredible scenery and the beauty of all of it to Sarah so that she could "see" it in her mind.

They unloaded their bags in the hotel lobby and checked in. Once in their room, Kendra opened the blinds and the view took away her breath.

"Oh, Kendra! This is the most wonderful thing to ever happen to me!"

"Sarah, there is a chance that the doctors can not help you, but if they cannot restore your sight, maybe they can at least stop the deterioration and you won't get any worse. If you stay as you are, at least you can see a little bit. Please don't build your hopes too high because you may be disappointed."

"I won't, sis. If all that happens is that I got to come to this beautiful country, then that will be almost as good. So don't worry about me. I'll be fine with whatever the outcome is."

The next morning and during the days to follow, Sarah was subjected to test after test after test on her eyes. Kendra waited patiently for her in the surgery waiting room as a team of doctors surrounded the little girl day and night in constant probes, questions and x-rays. Finally, the decision was made to try surgery. If successful, Sarah would have normal eyesight, but if unsuccessful, she would be totally blind. A delicate surgery requiring about twelve hours, the little girl would be strapped down so as to be perfectly still the entire twelve hours. One movement could cause instant blindness. Sarah was briefed on all that was required of her and nothing was held as to the seriousness of the operation. Sarah nodded agreement and understanding of the terms as they were told to her. Dr. Thornton was completely captivated by the sweetness and maturity of this little girl. He wanted more than anything else to help her.

The night before the surgery, Kendra called her folks.

"Mom, I want you and Dad and the children to put Sarah on your devotional prayer list for the next several weeks. She is in grave danger of losing what eyesight she has left. Please pray for the success of it and that she may see."

"We will, Kendra. Your father has already put her name on our prayer list. The girls and even Sammy have also requested it."

"Thanks, Mom. Do you want to talk to Sarah?"

"Put her on."

"Hi, Mom-Number-Two. Don't worry about me. I am all right with whatever the outcome is. I think I can play the piano without eyes if I have to! If I can't, Kendra will be my eyes!"

"Okay, honey, take care and you're on our prayer list. We love you."

The night seemed to drag on as Kendra and Sarah lay awake talking about the events of the next day. Kendra was terrified for Sarah, but couldn't let the little girl know that anything was wrong.

At the same time, Sarah really *was* terrified, but couldn't let her big sister know just how scared she really was.

So both of them held their feelings at bay and talked into the night of other things.

"Wonder how Dumpling is doing without us?"

"Oh, Kendra, she *is* probably sad."

"You know, we really need to get some rest now. Goodnight, Sarah."

"Goodnight, sister."

Morning came too soon and the two girls got up and dressed and went down to breakfast. Sarah was allowed only liquids so she just drank some juice. Kendra just couldn't seem to get anything to go down, so both left and went to the hospital to check in.

As soon as Sarah was prepped for surgery and given the necessary sedative, Kendra was instructed to wait out the next twelve hours in the surgery waiting room.

There she would be served lunch and dinner so that she would not have to leave the room and take a chance that the doctor would come out to talk to her and find her gone. She hugged her new little sister and told her how dearly she loved her and Sarah was wheeled from her sight.

Kendra curled up on the divan in the waiting room and closed her eyes. Her prayers and thoughts were for Sarah, a dear little girl who, as a baby had been taken from her biological mother because of the father's physical abuse of the little girl. Sarah's biological mother and daddy had never married, and the father's continual slapping the baby caused her blindness after she was struck on the head.

Although she was considered blind, Sarah could see shadows and some movement but could not make out details. With this handicap, it was even more astounding that she was such a talented musician. When Mr. and Mrs. McCullough, although up in years, wanted to adopt the little girl, it was with eagerness the birth mother had given her up, not willing to be tied down to a near-blind child. Now with the deaths of the McCulloughs, the Tinkers adopted her and hoped to fulfill their dream——-that Sarah could regain her eyesight!

A lady came and sat down by Kendra and began to talk. Kendra did not feel like talking because she wanted to think. She pulled the blanket up over her head, hoping the woman would get the hint. In the darkness under the blanket, Kendra could see Keith. Why didn't he love Sarah like she did? Was he jealous of her? And she had thought that if she stayed married to Keith, they could adopt her as theirs. She was glad that her parents had adopted her. Keith was so unpredictable, who knows what he might do.

Kendra's mind began to whirl around and around with all that had transpired in such a short time. Not many months beforehand, she was singing and twirling around her bedposts in anticipation of a date with Keith Kouch. The pictures and memories of their honeymoon cottage and the happiness of those days, etched forever in her mind, Kendra fell asleep under the hospital blanket right there in the waiting room.

"Mrs. Kouch, wake up. You've been asleep almost twelve hours!" An aide was shaking Kendra by the shoulders when she bolted upright, wide-eyed and heart pounding.

"Sarah? How is Sarah?"

"The doctor wishes to speak with you now."

Kendra threw back the cover and jumped up to meet Dr. Thornton as he came into the room.

"Kendra, I have good news! Sarah's eyesight is restored! She will have to be perfectly still for yet another twelve hours. For this reason, we will keep her eyes taped shut and her wrists and ankles secured so that there will be no movement. She's a determined little girl so I know she can do this!"

Without even giving it a second thought, Kendra threw her arms around a startled doctor and hugged him with all her heart.

"Oh, thank you, thank you, thank you!" And whispering she said, "And thank you, God!"

"I'm just as tickled as *you*. She did very well and the damage was repairable after all. If this could have been done right after it happened, she wouldn't have gone all these years seeing only movement and shadows. I'm very happy for her and for you, too."

"May I see her?"

"She is still in recovery. I suggest you go up to her room and wait for her. It will be another couple of hours before she gets back up there. You just be there when she opens her beautiful blues. She's going to be so happy!"

Kendra gathered up her belongings and went up to the third floor room where Sarah had left her things. She pulled up the recliner and sat beside the bed to wait.

She thought to herself how often lately she had sat at the bedside of those she loved. She remembered to call her mother and thinking of the time difference, she decided to call her anyway. No matter the time, her mother and daddy and siblings would want to know Sarah's fate.

"Hello, Mom! Sarah is in recovery! The operation was a success!" Kendra bubbled her happiness over the phone and Nell wished she were there to rejoice with her.

"That's wonderful, Kendra! We'll all *be so happy!* Do you know how much longer you'll be there before you can come home?"

"Not yet. But I will let you know. I'll hang up now; I'm expecting her back in the room in a little while and I want to be here. I love y'all."

"Love you, too, dear. Bye."

Kendra turned her thoughts back to Keith. She had not seen him since two weeks before she left. Edwina told her mother that he was miserable missing her and counting the days until she could come home. She didn't know whether she would go see him immediately upon her return or not. She wanted to give him time to cool down and to think of all he needed to change about his life.

The door opened and the nurses pushing the gurney with the little girl on it, came in. She was lying perfectly still and her eyes were taped shut.

"Sarah?"

"Kendra, that you?"

"Sure is. I hear you did great!"

"I did?"

"Did the doctor tell you?"

"He said you'd want to tell me the news!"

"Well, little sister, you are going to *see*! Now don't get too excited and move around. You must be very still for twelve more hours, then the tape comes off. You're going to get to see what your new big sister looks like and you can see your new little sisters and brother and your new mother and your new father and Dumpling and..."

Kendra realized she was rattling on and on and as she looked at Sarah, a smile crossed the little girl's lips and she fell asleep. Kendra kissed her on the cheek as the gurney was moved into place and secured. The nurse left and Kendra once again took up a vigil at Sarah's bedside.

The next morning around 9:00, when the twelve hours had passed, the team of doctors came into Sarah's room.

"It's time to take off the tape, little girlfriend, and let you see the world!"

Sarah was giggly and excited as the tape was slowly removed. Kendra held her breath as the last tape was peeled away.

"Open your eyes, Sarah."

Sarah's eyelids fluttered like a delicate butterfly trying to fly for the first time, and she opened her eyes. She squinted from the light and slowly opened them wider, then wider, all the while looking around the room slowly trying to absorb what all she saw there. The room was deathly quiet as though it were holding its breath.

"Kendra, my sister! You are beautiful!"

"Oh, Sarah, Sarah, I am so happy!" The two girls embraced as the streams of tears wet their faces and necks. The doctors and nurses in the room wept unashamedly at the happiness of the two girls.

"She can be dismissed to go home in about one more week," Dr. Thornton told them. "There's no follow up necessary and she can go about a normal life now without having to worry. However, you must never get an extremely hard blow to the skull again. In that case, the blindness *could* return."

The airplane, on which Kendra and Sarah traveled, landed in Oklahoma City at Will Rogers Airport exactly three weeks since it carried them to Germany. They were home! Nell and Kenneth and the children were at the airport gate to meet them when the plane landed. They ran out the gate into the waiting arms of the two girls as they came down the ramp.

All of them were talking at the same time, and Sarah was trying to see them all for the first time, and to memorize the faces that for so long, she had wanted to see. They linked arms and walked back through the gate and to the car.

"Sammy, you look so much older than I thought!" And Sammy glowed.

"Annanell and Abigail, you seem like twins! I have twin sisters! You're prettier than I ever imagined!" Sarah couldn't take her eyes away. Annanell and Abigail could only smile. The words just wouldn't come.

"And Momma Nell and Daddy Ken, I am so proud to be a part of this family. It is so good to *see* you, *really see you!*"

Once back home, Sarah was anxious to see her room and surroundings and most of all to sit at the baby grand piano and know what it was to see the keys as she played. Dumpling was curled up in a ball on the doormat waiting when they came in. Of course she didn't hear them, so she was startled when Kendra picked her up, but then recognizing her, she began to purr her happiness at having her home. The family stayed up all night getting acquainted through sight instead of sound and movement, and finished off the early morning hours with a devotional of thanksgiving. As the sun began to come up, the house finally grew quiet.

Twenty-three

Mr. Fuller called his congratulations and told Kendra to take another week off in order to get rested up before she and Sarah returned to work. Kendra was grateful because although she was happy for Sarah, she was extremely exhausted. And she knew that she would be facing Keith again and did not know what she would find.

With mixed emotions she and Sarah prepared for a ride over to the hospital to see Keith. She prayed to herself softly as she drove that he would be happy for Sarah and be glad to see her, too.

When she got to Keith's room, he was preparing to go to work out. He was being released on the weekend and there were a lot of instructions to give him for follow-up when he got home. He was excited to get to go home and so he was in an especially happy mood.

"Oh, baby, I am so glad to see you. I have missed you so much. It's been five weeks since I last laid eyes on you. Come here." Kendra walked to him in a sort of trance. He still held a control over her that she could not deny. Sarah stood in the doorway, quietly watching. Inching closer, she looked at Keith as one who had never seen him before. In a moment of horror, she screamed and ran from the room.

"Sarah! Wait! What's wrong? Honey, come back!"

"Let her go, Kendra. Come on over here and kiss me. I need you so much. You are going home with *me*, aren't you?"

"Not now, Keith, let me go to Sarah. What on *earth* is wrong with her?"

Keith reached out for Kendra's arm and pulled her to him. Now that he could walk, he held her tight until she struggled to get loose.

He pressed his lips against hers in his usual passionate way, and she pulled away.

"I can't think of us right now, Keith," she said and she ran from him to catch Sarah.

Sarah was crying hysterically and pacing back and forth as she waited for the elevator. Kendra grabbed her and hugged her tight.

"Whatever is wrong, Sarah? Tell me."

Between gulps of air and crying, Sarah managed to get out the words.

"Keith—he's the man in the picture—Kendra, he's my father! He's the one who caused my blindness in one of his temper fits!" And she became hysterical again. Kendra couldn't believe her ears, and in almost a state of shock, she managed to get Sarah on the elevator and out to the car. It was hard to drive home. Neither could see through the windshield for the tears.

In the days to follow, Kendra pieced together the story with the help of the papers the McCulloughs had left on Sarah's birth and adoption. A passionate and rebellious teen, and a teen who had to always prove to his father that he was a man, Keith had fathered a child when he was still almost a child himself. The girl chose to keep the baby and Keith had hated the little girl who was a reminder of the failure his father always thought he was. One day in one of his "moods" he had thrown the child against the wall and from then on, her sight had begun to dim. The mother had not wanted a blind child so she had given her up for adoption. The McCulloughs, in their desperation for a child had paid dearly to get her, but they had loved her beyond belief.

Kendra went to see Edwina. She begged her for help. Edwina was sorry that they never told anyone, but she told Kendra that was the reason they left Lawton. They wanted to get that part of their lives behind them. They knew that Keith had fathered a child out of wedlock, but he had restored his life to God and wanted a new start. It was all to be put behind him and forgotten.

"Cal and I thought that with *you*, he'd find that. You seemed to be all he needed to keep him on the 'straight and narrow.' We didn't know that Sarah was that child. We had lost touch with her and didn't intend to ever know what had happened to her, both for *our* sake and also for *hers*. I'm sorry, Kendra, so sorry.

"I know that Keith has problems, but with your love beside him, he will make it, I just know it. Please won't you stick by him and help him? He'll be coming home tomorrow; won't you be here to greet him?"

Kendra was stunned. *Greet* him? How could she? Their whole relationship had been a lie. How foolish she felt that she had kept her virginity for one who had not kept his. What a mockery of marriage! What lies! What deceit! How many times had she forgiven him only to be abused again...and again...? Would she be a fool to take him back? Or would she be a fool *not* to when he needed her so desperately? It seemed that only *she* could help him. What should she do? How many times does God forgive? How many times must *we* forgive? *How can I break my vows?* Questions and no answers plagued her all over again.

"Edwina, I don't know what to do." And Kendra left the dear lady in tears. It was sad enough that she had lost her husband, now she was losing a daughter-in-law, too. *How can I be so cruel?* Kendra thought as she too, left in tears.

That night, Kendra called the family together and told them she had made her decision.

"I will go help Keith check out of the hospital tomorrow morning, and we will, together come to terms that we can live with. I still love him with all of my heart." Sadly, she gathered Dumpling into her arms and climbed the stairs to her room that she shared with Sarah.

Sarah heard the muffled sobs into the pillow as Kendra cried herself to sleep. She was lost and did not know what to say to her new sister.

Saturday morning came and Kendra went to the hospital. She entered Keith's room and he was up and dressing to go home. It would be a while before he would be completely healed, but he had come a long way since that early morning of the accident.

"Hi, baby, I knew you'd come. Give me a kiss."

Kendra stood in the doorway and didn't move.

"I've done a lot of thinking and praying about us, Keith. Why didn't you tell me about Sarah? I could have forgiven you. Why didn't you tell me about your bouts with temper and temporary insanity when you were abusive and cruel? Knowing the problem, together we could have sought help, but no, you chose to hurt and abuse. I don't think you *want* to change. It's been a long and hard decision for me to make. I will probably always love you, and in order to show you how much I love you, I have decided to leave you. It's the only way you will ever get help. Maybe if your father had gotten help early in *his* marriage, things would've been different for *you*, and consequently, different *for us*. I have come to tell you goodbye." And she turned to walk out.

"Kendra! No! You can't do this to me! I love you! Doesn't that mean anything to you at all?"

"Of course it does, Keith, but it means nothing to *you*. By your actions, I have learned that you love no one but yourself. Putting me through all the obscene calls just to satisfy your selfish whim was cruel and vicious. You don't treat one you love that way. Knocking me down and injuring my wrists for only trying to love you, and keeping the fact from me that you had a little girl that you injured with your cruelty was dishonest and deceitful. I could have forgiven you, especially if I had known you wanted to do better and were at least, trying. If I stay with you, will I eventually be injured to the point of blindness, too? My hands and wrists were injured to the point of affecting my music.

"You allowed me to find out about the child by hurting Sarah who had already been through enough. Your actions are sadistic and no one who loves you is safe from you. No *one*, or no *thing*—not even an innocent kitten.

"You had me so awestruck that I had actually convinced myself that the cruelty to me was *my* fault. You could even make me believe those things never happened.

"It took Millie's death to wake me. You fooled me along for quite a while. It must make you feel proud that you could deceive a naïve little girl like me who didn't know any better, that you could bend everything into whatever you wanted it to be.

"I think I've grown up more this last year than at any other time in my life. I'm just so sorry that it has to be this way. We could have had it *all*. Yes, I will always love you—there will never be anyone who loves you like I do—but I won't stay married to you. Happy marriages are built on mutual respect and kindness, not deceit and cruelty. Goodbye, Keith."

Keith stood leaning against the bed rail, totally astounded at what he'd just heard. When it sunk in, Kendra was out the door. He stumbled trying to catch her and called out: "Kendra, Kendra! Come back! I'll make it up! I'm sorry! Please, baby, please!"

His pleading tugged at Kendra's heartstrings again, and she stopped a moment in the hall, listening to his plea. She took a few steps, hesitated, and stopped again. Her eyes filled with tears and just as she started to turn around and go back, Keith called out: "Kendra! You know you can't leave me. You're breaking your vows! You don't believe in divorce, little girl, so get yourself right back here, this minute!"

The veins in his neck stood out and the familiar beads of perspiration broke out on his upper lip and his face was turning red. Kendra was in the hall and didn't see it, but she knew by the tone of his voice, it was there.

The memories of it were now vivid in her mind and no longer seemed a figment of her imagination as they once had when she was blinded by her love for him. For just a second, she stopped. Then, not hesitating this time, she straightened up, wiped her eyes, and slowly began to walk. Faster and faster, she picked up the gait until she stepped out of the hospital and into the bright sunlight. She looked up at the clear, blue sky and taking a deep breath, she inhaled the crisp clean air, and ran to her car.

Meet Molly Lemmons

Molly Lemmons has been telling stories all of her life. Only in the last few years has she become a professional story teller and a published author of her first book, *Kind of Heart*. She has been published in numerous magazines as well as the *Chicken Soup For the Soul* series, and her newspaper column ran for three years in Oklahoma, Texas, and Arkansas papers. She is an alumnus of Oklahoma Christian University and has worked for the Mustang Public Schools for twenty-two years. She has two grown children, Roger and Lucinda, two grandchildren, and six cats.

VISIT OUR WEBSITE
FOR THE FULL INVENTORY
OF QUALITY BOOKS:

http://www.wings-press.com

Quality trade paperbacks and downloads
in multiple formats,
in genres ranging from light romantic
comedy to general fiction and horror.
Wings has something
for every reader's taste.
Visit the website, then bookmark it.
We add new titles each month!